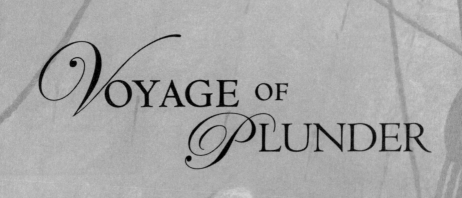

VOYAGE OF PLUNDER

MICHELE ❧ TORREY

VOYAGE OF PLUNDER

CHRONICLES OF COURAGE

Alfred A. Knopf
New York

VOYAGE OF PLUNDER

Being the true story of my, Daniel Markham's,

capture by pirates, of my misadventures

in distant parts of the world,

and finally, of my falling into wicked ways,

for which I suffered dreadfully.

As told to
MICHELE   TORREY

My sincere thanks once again to Ron Wanttaja for his assistance with all things nautical. His eagle eye and suggestions helped make the manuscript "shipshape." All opinions expressed in this book are solely mine. If there are any remaining errors, whether nautical or otherwise, they remain my responsibility alone, as to write a story of this nature it is often necessary to perform a balancing act between "fact" and "fiction."

THIS IS A BORZOI BOOK PUBLISHED BY ALFRED A. KNOPF

Copyright © 2005 by Michele Torrey
Jacket illustration copyright © 2005 by Donato Giancola

www.randomhouse.com/kids

Library of Congress Cataloging-in-Publication Data
Torrey, Michele.
Voyage of plunder / Michele Torrey. — 1st ed.
    p.   cm.
SUMMARY: Fourteen-year-old Daniel's life is turned upside down when his father's merchant ship is plundered by pirates in 1696 and Daniel is forced to stay aboard the pirate ship as a hostage. Includes bibliographical references (p.).
ISBN 0-375-82383-2 (trade) — ISBN 0-375-92383-7 (lib. bdg.)
[1. Pirates—Fiction. 2. Sea stories.] I. Title.
PZ7.T645725Vp2005   [Fic]—dc22   2004020424

Printed in the United States of America

July 2005

10 9 8 7 6 5 4 3 2 1

First Edition

To Carl,
for walks in the snow
and middles

Come, all you brave boys, whose courage is bold,
Will you venture with me? I'll glut you with gold.
Make haste unto Corona: a Ship you will find,
That's called the FANCY, will pleasure your mind.

Captain Every is in her, and calls her his own;
He will box her about, boys, before he has done.
French, Spaniard, and Portuguese, the heathen likewise,
He has made a war with them until that he dies.

—"A Copy of Verses,
Composed by Pirate Captain Henry Every"
(1696)

CHAPTER

I

There are few men in this world who can say they have seen their father die twice. God's truth, I might be the only one.

Mine is not a pretty tale, but it begs telling nonetheless. It begins when I was three years old, after my mother died.

When the men started coming to our home . . .

They slipped in and out like ghosts, shadows dancing from wall to wall. They talked in low whispers with my father. If the weather was warm, I would lie in my bed and listen to the whispers. For me, it was a comforting sound, like the water in Boston Harbor as it caresses the shore. But if the weather was cold, wintry, I would cry when left alone, my tears turning to ice, the heat from the warming pan long gone. One of the men would scoop me up, blankets and all, and carry me to sit before the roaring fire.

My favorite was Josiah Black. Ofttimes he sat me on his lap as I alternately turned my gaze from Josiah to the fire and back to Josiah again, pulling my blanket close. Josiah was tall. His skin was pale, his nose strong and sharp, his hair black and shining as a crow's feathers. His eyes were like wells of ink, and he smelled of tobacco and rum. It fast became my favorite smell.

On these nights, my father would finally say, "Do you not think Daniel should go to bed? 'Tis past the midnight hour."

Puffing contentedly on his long pipe, Josiah would reply, "There will be time for sleep later. Let the boy stay."

When I was seven years old, too big to be sitting on anyone's lap, Josiah Black took me to a hanging. I'd never seen a pirate hanged before.

There were three of them. I knew they were evil men— wicked to the core, doomed, for I'd heard it at the meetinghouse the Sunday last. I clenched Josiah's hand and watched the pirates kick the empty air, wondering if they could already see the gaping jaws of hell and the everlasting lake of fire.

When finally they hung still, and after I was done staring, I tugged on Josiah's hand. "I'm hungry."

But he seemed not to remember I was there, instead staring at the bodies that spun slowly on their ropes. His grip on my hand was like iron, his face hard.

We stood there a long time before Josiah said, "Come, Daniel, my boy," and we went home to a meal of codfish chowder, bread, cheese, quince tarts, and ale. Josiah watched me as I ate, saying to my father, "Hanging brings out the hunger in Daniel."

There were other men besides Josiah, of course, men who stirred the shadows, whispering among themselves, sometimes peering anxiously out the window at a gathering storm. But by morning, like as not, none remained except myself, my father, and our few servants. The walls were silent. The men were gone. We were alone again.

The air outside my coverlet was often freezing. After my father would awaken me, he'd press me to his bosom, tickle my nose, and tell me to rise and shine like a good lad. Then I would race to the kitchen hearth to sit in the chair at the chimney side, my feet scorched by the snapping fire, my front sizzling, my back shivering. And I would open my hand to inspect a trinket one of the men had given me the night before. A carved piece of ivory. A fancy coin. A tooth of gold. A pearl. A child's ring.

I had many such treasures.

Somehow I believed life would carry on so. That although the years would pass, nothing would change—the nights always filled with whispers, with ghosts, the mornings filled with treasure.

But all things change.

It began at the meetinghouse one Sunday in the form of a woman named Faith. The year was 1694, and I was twelve years of age. Faith was just a few years older than me. Sixteen, I think. On this day, I sat with the other boys on the gallery stairs. It was November, and I could see my breath. My hands and feet had frozen into lumps. But I dared not stamp my feet nor rub my hands together. If I did, I could be sure of a sharp rap on the head from the watchful deacon, whose duty it was to rap boys on the head. So I just breathed hard and watched the clouds of breath from all of us boys, like fog in the harbor.

My father sat by himself in a pew. The pews were of the hardest wood, straight-backed, meant for keeping one awake. They were divided into squares, and my father had the best pew square in the meetinghouse, directly before the pulpit. The Seating Committee had assigned it to him because he was a goodly man, the wealthiest, and had once been married to the governor's daughter. My father's name was Robert Markham, and he was a merchant. On that Sunday he wore a powdered periwig, its voluminous curls lending my balding father both warmth and dignity.

(Just that morning, while we were getting ready for Sunday meeting, my father had called for me; he had misplaced his spectacles and needed help finding them. After a bit of searching, I found them tucked in the curls of his periwig! We shared a hearty laugh, and I warmed despite the frosty air. "Ah, Daniel," my father had finally gasped, his eyes sparkling with tears of laughter as he drew me into a fatherly embrace, "whatever would I do without you?")

Now, at the meetinghouse, at the start of the sermon's second hour, the commotion began. If it could be called a commotion. A cough, weak and delicate, coming from the women's section. It was Faith Grey. (No one can leave during meeting, not unless one is dying. And so Faith coughed.) Heads turned. The minister frowned. The sermon paused, started, paused. I was relieved by such an interruption. I rubbed my hands and stamped my feet and the deacon didn't notice, so upset was he by all the head turning.

Then Faith stopped coughing. But even though she stopped, one head kept turning—my father's. Every few seconds he turned to look at her, not seeming to care that the minister frowned and the sermon faltered once again. I could tell by the sinking of my heart that things were about to change. And they did.

A year later, Faith Grey and Robert Markham were married, and Faith moved into our house. Immediately the men stopped coming. There were no more whispers, no more treasures, no more Josiah Black.

I hated Faith.

Skin pasty white, hair mousy brown, eyes not even brown or green but in between and so nothing at all. Plain, plain, plain was Faith. What my father saw in that drab mouse I cannot say.

She pretended to be my mother, once calling me "son," smiling her drab smile. I told her not to call me "son," that she was not my real mother. My *real* mother . . . Abigail, the daughter of the former governor of Massachusetts. Abigail, who died of fever when I was three years old. I had vague memories of my mother's arms wrapped around me, the brush of her lips against my forehead.

I knew my real mother was beautiful, for I had a golden locket with her miniature and I had been told many times by my father while he sat by the fire with that wistful look in his eye. My mother had eyes the color of the ocean, like my own. Tawny hair streaked with gold—the color of a sunset—like my own. A smile that was not drab like Faith's, but full of laughter and ease. A straight nose—a heavenly nose, my father called it—so unlike that round nothing-nose Faith was always blowing, raw, moist, and tipped with pink.

Often, I stared at my mother's miniature, imagining what she would look like if she were still here. She would look nothing like Faith, of that I was certain. I snapped the locket shut and pressed it against my lips.

Now, when school let out for the day, I did not return home until late.

Instead, I visited my mother's grave in the churchyard. I knelt, the tombstone cold and gritty under my fingers, telling her things I would not tell another. I told her my secrets and my sorrows. About Josiah, wondering where he was and whether I would see him again. About my father loving Faith now.

Once, lying beside her grave, I fell asleep; hours later I awakened, much stiffened.

The wildflowers I'd laid on the grassy mound were already wilting. I sat up, stretching, surprised to discover that someone had covered me with a cloak while I'd slept. And lingering on the fibers of the wool was the scent of tobacco and rum.

Josiah?

I jumped to my feet, casting my gaze about. The tombstones. The trees rustling in the evening breeze, pink blossoms falling gently like snow. The church with its towering steeple. "Josiah?" I said aloud.

But, alas, there was nothing.

Nothing but the beat of my heart.

In my fourteenth year, I began apprenticing at my father's place of business.

It was located at the wharf, the sign reading ROBERT G. H. MARKHAM, MERCHANT. Inside it was cramped and cluttered. It smelled of beeswax polish, wood smoke, tobacco, and ale. I enjoyed working there because then I could be with my father without Faith around. I could pretend that everything was the way it used to be.

One day I sat at my desk beside the fire and watched as my father conducted his business. Beneath his wig, his features were soft, rounded, for he loved rich foods and fine ales. He talked with customers, with ships' captains, added columns of numbers with a flourish of his quill pen. I grew drowsy.

"Done with your work, Daniel?"

I jerked my head up off my desk, realizing with a start that all the customers had left. Outside the panes of leaded glass, it was dark. I must have dozed.

"Not quite. I'll be finished in a moment." Embarrassed to have been caught napping, anxious to please my father, I stifled a yawn and reached for my last bit of paperwork, rubbing a dent on my cheek where my quill had made an impression.

I studied the parchment for a moment, puzzled, still half groggy with sleep. It was a ship's manifest—a list of cargo: iron ingots, sugar, gold, jewels, silks . . . A princely treasure certainly, but that was not what caught my attention; it was the ship's name: *Norfolk*.

I arose from my chair and approached my father. "Wasn't the *Norfolk* looted by pirates a few months back?"

"Eh?" He looked up from what he was doing.

"Wasn't the *Norfolk* looted by pirates? The news was all over Boston."

He frowned as if not remembering.

I held the parchment in front of his face. "Then why would we have its manifest?"

He took the document from me, studied it briefly, then put it aside. "I'll take care of it later."

"But why—"

"Daniel, please. Not now. Pray be a good boy and listen to me. I must have a word with you about something else." He paused, glancing at me before looking away. "I've made a decision, son."

I held my breath, suspecting that things were about to change again, as at the meetinghouse two years before.

Digging in his pocket, he pulled out his snuff box and handkerchief. He inhaled a pinch of snuff, sneezed, wiped his nose, then cleared his throat, his eyes a little watery. "Now then. Daniel, you're a smart lad, and I'm sure you'll understand that this is difficult for me to say. Please don't make it harder than it already is. You see, Daniel, your mother and I—"

I stiffened. "She's not my mother."

For a few moments he said nothing, shuffling a few papers about his desk before turning back to me with a sad look on his face. "Yes. Well. I have decided that matters have become much too difficult here in Boston."

"What do you mean?" My chest squeezed, and I felt as if I could not breathe.

"What I mean is," he said, giving my shoulder a pat, "Faith is to have a child. Daniel, it sorrows me to tell you this, but I've decided that your mother's health is too weak for the northern winters. She's of a delicate constitution. Therefore, come the end of the week, we'll be leaving Boston, just the three of us. There is a plantation in Jamaica that my agent has secured—"

But I heard no more. I brushed my father away and fled the room. I don't remember opening the door, except there was a blast of cold air and suddenly I was outside. Running. Past the wharf, down the streets, dogs yapping at my heels.

Faith.

I hated her.

CHAPTER

2

At the water's edge, a cage dangled from a gibbet.

I stared, shuddering in horror.

It was the first day of December, 1696, and I stood at the rail of my father's ship, the *Gray Pearl,* as she sailed out of Boston Harbor, past Bird Island.

The cage was shaped like a man, with head and shoulders tapering down to the feet. Inside the cage, a corpse rotted. The body was tarred, banded with ribs of iron. Ravens pecked at what flesh they could find while the cage slowly rotated round and round, metal grating.

Empty sockets stared back at me. The lips were gone. Teeth gleamed. I glimpsed bleach-white bone. Strands of hair. A scrap of tattered clothing.

It was a pirate.

Executed and doomed to rot as a warning for all.

Out on the open waters, the wind stiffened, blowing from our starboard quarter. As the captain had predicted, we made good speed. I felt a lump in my throat as the land grew smaller and smaller, as we left behind everything I had ever known. Boston . . . my home . . . a thread of black upon the horizon.

Fare thee well, Mother.

I ignored my father's invitation to join him for supper and instead went below to my cabin. I had been to sea once before, when I was just four, maybe five years old. I remembered it as a wooden world of laughter and sunshine, sailors and yarns and sitting perched upon my father's shoulders. But it was nothing like that now. The constant heaving, rolling, and seesawing back and forth made my head spin and my stomach queasy. By the end of the second day my cabin smelled foul, reeking of my insides.

Every few hours, my father begged me to come on deck, saying the fresh air would revive me. But I turned my face away.

Three times per day a sailor brought me food, emptied my bucket, and replaced the candle in the hanging lantern if it burned low. The lantern casing was metal, punched with holes. The pinpricks of light did little to chase away the darkness. Always I was starving and gobbled every scrap of food, but always it came back up. Afterward, I lay on my narrow bunk, exhausted, clasping my locket, tears stinging my eyes.

That Faith had bewitched my father, I had little doubt.

I had heard of such things—of witches casting spells to snag a husband, tricking the husband into doing whatever she wished. I knew that in his right mind, my father would *never* have left Boston. After all, not only was he a holder of the best pew square at the meetinghouse, but he owned a fleet of ships, including the

Gray Pearl. In short, he was a very important man. Why, then, would he suddenly move to Jamaica? It made no sense. Except that he was under a spell.

And so on our third day at sea, when my father entered my cabin, I felt it my duty as a good son to tell him. "Faith is a witch," I said, my voice as raspy as two stones rubbed together, "and you are under her spell. Why else would you have left Boston?"

"Daniel, I don't expect you to understand. But trust me, please trust me; this is for the best. Now, I want you to forget this nonsense about—"

"You don't care about Mother anymore."

A shadow of hurt crossed my father's face, like the passing of a cloud. He said nothing, merely studying my face for a few moments. Then he left, latching the door softly behind him.

I turned toward the wall. Pinpoints of lantern light streaked back and forth, like stars falling. Tears pressed hot against my eyes, but I refused to let them fall. Instead, I clenched my jaw, longing for the days before Faith had ruined everything. Days when it was just my father and me and the many men.

The next morning the cry of "Sail ho! Off the port quarter!" pealed through the ship. At first I rolled over and tried to ignore it. Then from above my head came the command of "All hands! All hands on deck! Ready about! Stations for stays!" Then the running of feet and the thump of tackle.

Why would there be such a commotion over the sighting of a ship? Weren't ships common enough? After all, this was the Atlantic.

Suddenly tired of my cabin, I sat up. My head reeled. I gritted my teeth and climbed out of my bunk, slipping on my breeches and a cotton shirt and vest. After hurriedly braiding my hair in a queue and then pulling on my stockings and silver-buckled shoes, I donned my cocked hat and staggered onto the upper deck. My eyes watered in the freshening breeze.

The rising sun shattered the cloud-studded sky with rays of yellow and orange. Halfway between the sun and the horizon, sails floated like the wings of a bird in flight. Below, a dark hull aimed toward us like a dagger.

"Look lively now, lads!" bellowed the captain through his speaking trumpet.

Sailors ran around me, their bare feet slapping the deck. One burly man knocked into me, scarcely apologizing as he ran by. I suddenly felt awkward. Stupid. Only fourteen years of age, average height, with soft muscles and pale skin, no doubt reeking like a rat in a cellar. I was in their way, knowing nothing of what they were doing. Hundreds of hempen ropes snaked this way and that. *How in the devil do they know which one to pull?*

"Ready! Ready! Ease down the helm!"

I spied my father on the quarterdeck. I began to make my way toward him but then hesitated, remembering his expression of hurt the day before. *But, I told myself, it was my duty as a good and faithful son to tell him of his bewitching. Now, perhaps, he will see Faith for what she is. He will return to Boston and get rid of her.*

With that thought, I squared my shoulders, climbed the companionway, and joined my father at the rail. "What is it?" I hoped he would say we were turning around and going home.

"You must be feeling better."

"I am," I replied, realizing I *was* feeling better, even though the *Gray Pearl* now rolled heavily through the swells. "What is it?" I asked again.

He handed me his spyglass.

It took me a moment to find her. A solitary three-masted ship headed our way, yards straining to every stitch of canvas.

"Could be nothing," my father was saying, "but she changed course to intercept once she spotted us. I told the captain to alter course and keep our distance."

"Why?" I lowered the glass, noticing my father's hands as he gripped the rail. His knuckles were white, and it looked as if he might snap the rail in half.

Then he was staring at me oddly. Sweat dotted his upper lip. "If anything happens, Daniel, promise me you'll look after Faith."

My knees felt weak. Something was not right, something my father was not telling me.

"Promise me, Daniel," he said again.

How could I make such a promise? I despised Faith. But then again, how could I refuse? I loved my father. "I promise," I said, pretending to mean it. I raised the glass and looked out to sea, feeling a sudden urge to apologize, to say I was sorry for calling Faith a witch. But I could not. I would not. Instead, I asked, "Are they pirates?"

"Pray they are not, Daniel. For the love of God, pray they are not."

The other ship drew nearer throughout the day. My father told me that the wind favored her, and to go below and look after Faith, that they would soon be upon us, for better or for worse. I was angry to be sent below. I started to tell my father that I was a child no longer, but I remembered my promise and bit my tongue.

When we had first boarded the ship in Boston, the captain had given his cabin to my father and Faith. (It was only right, seeing as my father owned the ship and was very important, besides.) Now Faith lay on the bed in the captain's cabin, her pregnancy as yet scarcely noticeable. Her skin looked green.

While I stood in the doorway, she groaned, rolled over, and retched into a bucket.

I slumped into a chair with a sigh. All of the excitement would be happening on deck while I played nursemaid. And I was feeling sick again. My father was right. Being belowdecks was bad for the head. Even worse was listening to someone else be sick. I clenched my teeth.

Half an hour . . .

An hour . . .

Again the running of feet. Commands barked through the trumpet. A slight change in course.

A nearby *boom!*

My heart lurched. *Cannon! So it is pirates! It has to be! Why else would someone fire upon a merchant ship?*

Then it seemed everyone was running and yelling at once—a thunder of feet above my head. I could not tell what was happening. Were we preparing to fire our cannon? Were the pirates aboard and attacking us all? Meanwhile, Faith was sitting up, reaching for me. "What's happening? Daniel, oh dear God, what's happening? My husband—my dear husband—"

Another boom.

Whump!

A crunch of wood.

"Dear God! Daniel! Tell me what's—" But before Faith could finish her sentence, she was vomiting again.

And then I heard them. The pirates. A clash of screams pierced the air, mixed with a screeching wail of trumpets, violins, drums, flutes. Hair prickled on the back of my neck. Panicked, I glanced about the captain's quarters. I needed some sort of weapon to defend us.

The captain's desk. I opened it. Logbook, papers, quills, ink pots, maps . . .

The screams were beside us now. The ships collided with a crunch, throwing me to my knees. The *Gray Pearl* leaned slightly, her timbers groaning. I tasted fear, my heart wild as a galloping horse.

"Daniel!" Faith had crawled out of bed and now clutched my arm. "Pray tell me. I must know."

"It's—it's pirates." I continued rifling madly through the desk. There. A dagger of some kind, rusted and bent. It would have to do. I stuffed it in the waist of my breeches.

So there we stood, Faith and I, waiting. Listening to the shrieks and the thumps and the explosions. Watching the door. Dreading when it would smash open and a huge pirate would fill the gap. I glanced at her, wondering if I looked as scared as she did. Her hair was wild. The whites showed all around her pink-rimmed eyes. Tears hovered. Her chest heaved with panting.

Suddenly I felt sorry for her, witch or not. I would not want to be a woman when pirates attacked. For that matter, I would not want to be a boy either. Much as I hated to admit it, in that moment I was very much a boy—a frightened fourteen-year-old boy with a bent dagger in his waistband.

Suddenly everything turned quiet. Deathly quiet.

Then I smelled it. The stench of smoke. The nightmare of every sailor. My voice shook, "The ship is afire. We can't stay down here or we'll burn alive."

She nodded. A tear slid down her cheek.

I said a quick prayer as we left the cabin, her hand locked in mine.

CHAPTER
3

$\mathcal{F}$aith and I stumbled onto the upper deck. The smoke was thick and black. I coughed and gagged, pulling Faith along. Behind us was the roar of fire.

I could not see where I was going; I knew only that we had to get off the ship. But the *Gray Pearl* appeared deserted. *Where is everybody?* "Father!" My voice choked.

Then I heard voices ahead. A grunt of pain. "This way," I said to Faith, hurrying in the direction of the voices. The smoke began to thin. I picked my way past the mainmast, then past the main hatch. We stepped out of the swirling smoke and into a nightmare.

A band of pirates surrounded my father. I could see him kneeling in the center. As I watched, frozen with horror, one of the pirates placed his pistol to the back of my father's head and pulled the trigger.

My father jerked, then fell in a heap.

Faith screamed.

I realized that I too was screaming. "Father!" That I was running toward the pirates, dagger in my hand, screaming, screaming. They turned in surprise, as if not knowing anyone else was aboard. Hands grabbed me. I think I cut one of them; I'm not sure. I was flailing. Screaming and flailing.

"Father!"

He lay in a pool of blood, his wig blown away.

"Father!"

They pinned me down. I could no longer move. Still screaming . . .

Screaming . . .

One of them calling my name. Over and over again.

"Daniel . . . *Daniel, my boy* . . ."

And I knew no more.

I wanted to stay in the darkness forever. A numbing darkness that knew no pain. A darkness that remembered only sitting on my father's lap, listening to the whispers, treasures locked in my hand.

Whenever the light threatened, I fled to the comfort of darkness, pulling it over me like a blanket. For with the light came knowledge. And I did not want to know. Not now. Not ever.

I don't know how long I stayed in the darkness. A few hours. A day. A week. It seemed only a moment. It seemed forever.

Then it was gone, like the tide receding, leaving me stranded.

And I was back in the light . . .

I lay on a bed in a cabin. A single candle's flame shone from a hanging lantern. It swayed with the movement of the ship. I knew immediately that I was not aboard the *Gray Pearl*. If I had been, I would have been dead, and I was not. Sadly, I was not. For wherever the *Gray Pearl* was, ashes scattered across the ocean, there also was my father. I longed to be with him. To have him back. To be anywhere except where I was now.

Beneath the lantern sat a man. He was the man who had pulled the trigger and killed my father. He was tall—even though he was sitting in the chair, I could tell that. He smoked a long pipe, and his hands were rough, callused, crisscrossed with scars. Grime edged his fingernails. His hair was plaited, bound with a strip of leather. He had a long, pale face, and as he smoked he watched me, his eyes pools of black in the candlelight. "You are awake," he said softly.

I said nothing, remembering.

"Hungry?" He pointed to a platter heaped with food. Steam rose in wispy curls. I smelled meat and spices and saw biscuits piled on the side.

I would have liked to turn away from the food. But he was right. I was hungry. Since boarding the *Gray Pearl* in Boston, I had vomited almost everything I had eaten. My stomach now felt like a cave. My limbs shook and my mouth watered. Slowly, I rose from the bed and sat at the table as far away from him as I could. I pulled the platter toward me and ate with my fingers. It burned my fingers and mouth, but I did not care.

"Something to drink?" He must have taken my silence for a yes, because he filled a goblet with a golden liquid. "It will make you feel better." He pushed it toward me across the table.

It was rum. Fumes swirled up my nose, and my eyes welled with tears. It burned my throat. I choked and gasped, and droplets flew. But I didn't care, and drank again.

He smiled. His teeth were straight, even, and white—a beautiful smile. It was unsettling, and so I looked away, swallowing.

"You always had a hearty appetite, Daniel, my boy."

I chewed louder, wishing to drown out the sound of his voice, wishing he would go away. For a while I ate in silence, the rum's warmth spreading through my body like blood dropped in water.

"You've grown." His voice was smooth, silklike. How I had always loved his voice.

I stuffed more food in my mouth and shut my eyes, stomach burning, wondering if I still had my dagger.

"I'm sorry. Really, I am. Forgive me, Daniel."

I opened my eyes and stared at him, stupidly. My head spun just a little. My mouth was stuffed with food. And then I began to laugh. It was a hysterical laugh, shrill and crazy-sounding. It burst out of me like poison. Food spilled out of my mouth and plopped onto my chest. I bumped my goblet with my elbow. Rum spread over the table and onto my lap. The goblet rolled to the floor with a clatter.

He stood, looking exactly as I remembered him. He moved toward the door, and then paused before opening it. "I did not know you were aboard. Believe me. It was the last thing I wanted you to see." Then he left, shutting the door behind him.

For a moment I just sat there, staring at the door, rum puddling on my lap. Suddenly I stood, roared, and hurled the platter at the door, laughing even harder when it splattered into a thousand million pieces of food. Ashes scattered across the ocean. I crawled among the bits of biscuits and beef, popping them into my mouth, laughing all the while.

Josiah Black is sorry. That's very funny.

My father had taught me to pray when I was very young. He'd showed me how to kneel beside my bed, how to fold my hands. Together we had prayed.

So I prayed now. I knelt beside the bed. I prayed for rescue, for death, for my father. I clasped my locket between my hands—my locket with my mother's likeness—and prayed she would beseech God on my behalf.

When I finally finished with "Amen," I waited for the heavens to answer me, for I was in desperate need. I had been betrayed by a man whom I had trusted. A man whom I had loved. A man who was a thief, a liar, a murderer. And not just an ordinary murderer, but a murderer of his friend. For my father had surely been Josiah's friend—as I had been. Now we both had been betrayed.

In the ship-creaking silence of the night, I clutched the bed-covers. It was horrible, this silence. *Why have I been left all alone? Why? Why? Why?* With a cry of rage, I pounded my bed with my fists. *Curse you, Josiah Black! Curse you forever! I swear to you upon my father's grave that I will see you hang!*

Then I began a most wretched weeping of a kind I'd never known before.

And during that time of weeping, I remembered.

Faith.

What has happened to her?

*I*t was no wonder Father's merchant ship the *Gray Pearl* had been captured by the pirate ship *Tempest Galley*. At 124 feet long, with twenty-six cannon and eight swivel guns mounted on her rails, the *Tempest Galley* had enough sail power to reach fourteen knots. That was as powerful and fast as a fifth-rate naval warship. Even with her sweeps alone—she had forty-six long oars—the vessel could reach three knots.

I knew many of the pirates aboard the *Tempest Galley*—not all, but many. There were, I think, 150 of them. I knew maybe thirty. They were the men who had visited my father's house so many times. Murderers, all of them. I despised them now, especially Josiah. I would not rest until I saw him hanged for piracy and murder.

One of the pirates told me that we were sailing around Africa to the Red Sea—"going on the Round," as they called it. He said the Red Sea teemed with ships laden with treasure, that finding treasure ships was as easy as dropping a bucket of pitch. They were off to make their fortunes, to bathe in jewels.

Of treasure, of jewels, I cared nothing. I cared only to get off the ship. But they ignored me when I demanded to be let off. One even said to jump overboard and swim if I wanted ashore that badly. They were off to become rich, and no one was going to stop them, not even little Daniel Markham.

Then, of course, there was Faith. I could not just leave her.

That first night, I had climbed on a chair and unhooked the lantern from the ceiling. I'd crept from my cabin, not overly careful to be quiet because a ship under sail makes all kinds of groaning and creaking and sloshing sounds.

Faith's cabin was the first I tried. I didn't let myself think of what would happen should it turn out to be the sleeping nest of a pirate. I was too tired to care. I just opened the door and peered in.

She was awake. She lay on the bed, blankets pulled to her nose, eyes saucers of fright. "Who is it?"

"It's me. Daniel."

"Daniel!" There was a rustle of clothing, and then she was beside me. Even in the dim lantern light I saw the splotches on her face. Her nose ran. Her eyes leaked. Everything about her was red and watery. "Daniel, oh, Daniel. Thank God you're not dead." So saying, she wrapped her arms around me, dropped her head on my shoulder, and sobbed.

That was the first night. After that, I'd taken a blanket and moved out of Josiah's cabin. Each night since, I'd slept in the hold. It was uncomfortable and swarmed with rats, but I would rather share my quarters with a rat than with Josiah.

On the third night, I was frightened. Faith's bedclothes were spotted with blood, and she seemed unnaturally pale. On this night, she didn't even weep. She merely lay there like a statue, eyes dry and unblinking.

"Faith!" I cried, rubbing her hand.

She did not answer me.

"Faith!"

It was strange. I no longer hated Faith. While having to defend her against pirates, while seeing her so scared, all my thoughts of witches seemed ridiculous. Even though she was not my mother and never would be, she was my father's wife— rather, his widow. He had loved her. And I had promised to protect her and care for her if anything happened to him, even though I didn't mean it at the time. Now that he was dead, I vowed to keep my promise.

I will not let Faith die.

I rubbed her hand, feeling helpless as a ship in stays, yet at the same time knowing what I must do. I had to convince Josiah Black to sail to port.

So, in the early morning, I went to Josiah.

I flung open the door to his cabin and marched in. Josiah— *Captain* Josiah, that is—lay atop his covers, his clothing unbuttoned and wrinkled, his shoes not even pulled off. Whiskers shadowed his face. His eyelids fluttered open. I waited until he focused on me, then announced, "My father's wife is dying. And it's all your fault."

He blinked a leaden blink, ran his tongue over cracked lips, and then tried to heave himself to his feet. A bottle clattered away, and he fell back. "Help me, Daniel, my boy."

But I did not. I stood with my arms crossed, hating him.

"You know," he said as he struggled to his feet, "I used to know a child who was kindhearted and who would help a poor man in distress."

I said nothing.

"'Tis a pity." Josiah stumbled out the doorway, lurching from side to side. Outside Faith's cabin door, he paused to button and smooth his waistcoat and breeches, then rapped lightly and entered. "Goodwife Markham. 'Tis I, Josiah Black, come to see to your well-being." And he latched the door behind him.

I waited, knowing that surely Josiah had to realize that Faith needed help. Anyone with sixpence of sense would know she might die unless she was taken ashore. This ship was no place for a lady, especially a lady with child.

"Well?" I said when Josiah finally emerged. "Are you going to port, or are you going to let her die?"

"It's not that simple, lad." He lurched his way back to his cabin, and I followed.

"What do you mean, it's not that simple? It's as simple as an order."

He didn't answer me right away. Instead, he withdrew four pistols from his sea chest and, after inspecting them, shoved them into his sash. Then, taking a cutlass from the chest, he thrust it into the air and slashed sideways. It was slightly curved, its hilt gleaming of gold. Seeming satisfied, he sheathed his cutlass into the scabbard that hung from his crossbelt. "Because, Daniel, my boy, a captain of the Brethren can give orders only in chase or battle. And since this is neither chase nor battle, I must instead call a meeting and a vote."

I was stunned. Of what use was a captain who couldn't give orders? "My father would never stand for such poppycock."

Upon my words, Josiah fixed me with a dark look. I forced myself to meet his gaze, wondering if he could see my eyelid twitch or my heart race.

I realized at that moment how little I knew Josiah Black.

They crawled out of every crevice of the ship.

Scars ran chin to ear to mouth, severing lips and breaking teeth. There were eye patches, tattoos, wooden legs. Fine clothes—velvets, laces, brocades—mixed with tattered rags, with kerchiefs knotted about their heads, and earrings of gold. Daggers, pistols, swords, gun belts hung everywhere.

They reeked of violence.

If only my father had known what kind of men these were.

"Go below, Daniel," ordered Josiah.

I looked at him towering above me, the top of my head no higher than his shoulder, his skin like alabaster no matter how fiercely the sun shone. "But I don't want to."

Josiah's voice hardened. "Go below. This is no place for a child. I shall take care of it, come what may."

"I am not a child."

Josiah sighed, exasperated. "Grow up then, if you must. But understand this, Daniel—I cannot save you from everything." With that, he drew a pistol and fired it into the air.

Where before there had been a stir of voices, now, except for the echo of pistol fire, there was silence. All the pirates faced Josiah, jammed in a circle around him. I smelled rum, beer, and stale sweat. I heard the sound of their breathing, the clink of their weapons. Melting into the bulwarks, away from Josiah's side, away from the circle's center, I suddenly wondered if Josiah was right. But, even as I wondered, I knew I had to stay. For Faith. For Father.

Josiah's voice was low and soft, yet it sliced through the air like his sword. "The woman is ill. She is with child and requires attention of a womanly sort. Newport is five days' sail—"

"Newport!" someone exclaimed. "But we've just sailed from Newport!"

"Five days' sail might as well be a year's sail," said a man with the wary look of a stray dog. "We're on the Round, Captain Black, and I don't know about anyone else, but I intend to stop for no one, sick or otherwise."

"Besides," said a pirate, greasy locks hanging beneath his kerchief, "she's seen too much for her own good, if you get my meaning. Once she's safe, she'll blabber. Women can't help but blab. It's in their nature."

"And I, for one," growled another, fingering the blade of his dagger, "will die before I dance the pirate's jig. There will be no hemp burn on the neck of this old buccaneer, and I'll kill anyone who tries."

A man pushed his way through the crowd, weapons clinking. A scar ran straight through his eyeball.

I unwittingly took a step backward.

"I say we cut her here," he said. "Women are bad luck."

Fear prickled my spine. *Cut her? Does that mean what I think it means?*

I had heard of pirates who ripped out the tongues of their captives and ate them with salt and pepper. Pirates who whipped and pickled people. Pirates who sewed the mouths of their victims closed because they talked too much. As a child, I had thought these mere tales of fancy. But now, I shivered.

I looked at Josiah. He said nothing, his eyes narrow and unreadable.

The scar-eyed man continued, "I knew a tar once who dressed his woman like a boy and brought her aboard 'cause he couldn't live without her. His ship vanished. Every mother's son of them—swallowed by the deep. Women—they're the devil's ballast."

They said more, but it was all the same. Women were bad luck aboard ships. Life at sea was dangerous enough. Women summoned monsters from the deep. They caused storms and shipwrecks. They made men stupid with jealousy, until they stabbed each other with pleasure and there was none left. Besides, they agreed, Faith had seen too much. And no one wanted to dance the pirate's jig, especially because of a woman.

With a rising horror, I saw it was hopeless.

They voted. Faith lost. Eight men versus 140 or some such.

Then it was as if something inside of me burst. Stars shot across the blackness of my mind, like on the day my father was killed.

I howled as a wild man, and God's truth, I felt rage enough to take on them all. I raced to the hatch and drew my dagger. My rusted, bent dagger.

"Touch her and I'll kill you!" I cried.

CHAPTER
5

*A*nd then the pirates laughed, holding their sides, wiping away tears.

When the laughter died away, the foremost pirate moved cheerfully toward the hatch, as if I'd told nothing but a jolly joke and he was the better for it. But I was not joking. I lunged for the man, swiping at him. I nicked him on the back of his hand and saw a crease of blood before he drew it away, his face darkening with rage. "Why, you—"

They held him back, laughing again.

"Blood and thunder, little Daniel's a fighter!"

"Full of piss and vinegar, that one!"

"He'll be one of us 'fore too long."

"I'll never be one of you!" I spat.

More laughter.

They were murderers, all of them. "My

father trusted you. He was your friend, and you murdered him. And now you want to murder his wife as well, and do God knows what else. I hate you. I hate all of you! I swear upon my soul you'll hang for killing my father!"

Suddenly the laughter died. Above my head the sails snapped with a shift in breeze. I swallowed hard, my breathing ragged.

One of the pirates stepped forward. Will Putt was his name. I remembered sitting on Will's lap when I was a child. Funny how I'd never realized how huge Will was until now. He was hairy-chested, and muscles bulged from places I never knew had muscles. He crossed his arms. "You have it wrong, Daniel. We trusted your father, and he betrayed *us.*" Will thumped his chest for emphasis as others nodded.

I blinked, not understanding.

"Your father purchased our goods—"

I glared at him. "Never! If he'd have known what kind of—"

Will held up his hand to silence me. "He knew. By God, boy, I'm telling you, he *knew.* For years he sold our stolen goods to the colonists. The colonists were only too eager to purchase our goods because there were no taxes, you see. Your father made a good living. He was a rich man. But he was rich because of us."

"You're lying!" Tears stung my eyes. I knew it wasn't true. It *couldn't* be true! "My father was a righteous man. He never would have—"

"A few months ago," said Will, "the government threatened to throw him in prison. To save his own hide, he turned king's evidence. Told them everything he knew. Our names, our faces, everything. So, you see, we had a score to settle. And there's a reward on all of our heads now because of him."

"But if you're telling the truth," I argued, "if he's been working with you for all these years, then why didn't the government threaten him with prison earlier? Why now?"

Will grinned, his eyes glittering. "Because, lad, a few months ago we looted the *Norfolk*. Worth a fortune, she was. A fortune belonging to the king. They could no longer look the other way and pretend nothing was happening. Heads had to roll, starting with your father's."

Will was wrong! *Wrong!* They all were! "But my father never did anything dishonest in his life. He was a *good* man! And he never would have done what you say he did. *Never!*" I said more, defending my father with every shred of honor, every shred of dignity I had remaining, beseeching all the pirates to believe me. Yet even as I spoke, a vague memory crawled in the back of my mind like a spider, long-legged, cobwebbed, and musty. *Norfolk . . . Norfolk . . .*

Finally, as each man except Josiah averted his eyes, my words trailed off. The ship settled into silence again, hemp groaning, water gurgling softly. My eyes welled with confusion and I hung my head, watching the deck shimmer through a curtain of tears.

Then it was as if I was speaking from far away, as if someone else had control of my voice, rather like a puppet on a string. "Sail to the nearest port," I said, my voice sounding as bleak as I felt. "Let Faith ashore, and I shall stay with you as your hostage. If Faith talks, kill me. She'll say nothing, I promise."

The wind cut through my clothing, and I shivered. Hair whipped into my eyes, and I wiped it away with a cold hand. I stared behind me into the blackness, rowing for the wharf, wishing the moon were visible, yet at the same time thanking my fortune that I was cloaked by darkness. No one had seen me.

I had escaped.

Just that morning—a morning of fat gray clouds and a nasty, wet wind—the *Tempest Galley* had anchored in Newport Harbor, bright pennants flying from her masts. As morning turned to midday, Faith was rowed ashore. I stood at the rail wondering when I would see her again, *if* I would see her again, still feeling the hot moistness of her hand against mine as she'd whispered good-bye and her eyes had fluttered closed.

After replenishing their water casks and food supplies—an easy task, as they had so recently reprovisioned—the pirate crew prepared to weigh anchor before the sun set. All of them fearing Faith might yap. All of them anxious to go on the Round. All of them imagining swimming in jewels.

Forty men circled the capstan, pushing the bars, singing lustily to the rhythmic clanking of the pawl. But then the wind shifted, the sky crackled with thunder, and their singing changed to curses. And while they swore (and while my ears burned with the vileness of it all), the tide turned against them. The *Tempest* tossed at her anchors. There would be no leaving tonight. Josiah and the others cursed their luck, but I prayed the wind would stay its course.

Shortly after the distant cry of midnight, I slipped away.

One does not keep promises with thieves and murderers. That I knew. I would tell the townspeople everything I had seen. I would tell them who had pulled the trigger and murdered my father. By morning, all the pirates would be in prison. Once they were tried and hanged and once Faith was cured of her illness, she and I would return to Boston, to my father's house. And there I would care for her and her child as my father had wished.

I just had not counted on it being so cold and windy.

The rowboat bumped against the wharf. It took me some fumbling minutes to tie it fast, but finally I succeeded and climbed out. My legs felt shaky, and the wharf seemed to bob before my eyes, ebbing and flowing. I crept along the wharf as best I could, anxious to make no sound, as the pirates might open fire from the ship if they suspected anything amiss.

See if they laugh at little Daniel Markham again, I thought as I picked my way over a fishnet. *I'll show them. I'll especially show you, Josiah Black.*

I was halfway down the wharf when, suddenly, a shape loomed beside me. A hand clamped over my mouth as an arm gripped my shoulders. Panic raced through my veins like ice water, and I struggled. *I am caught! The pirates must have been watching me!*

"Hush, you young fool," he whispered sharply in my ear. "I am your friend."

For a wild second, I wondered if I should bite his hand and shout anyway, but I decided not to be an idiot. If I shouted, all would be over. Besides, perhaps he was telling the truth. Perhaps he really *was* a friend. I ceased my struggling, and he slowly removed his hand. "Who are you?" I whispered.

"Not here," he replied. "Come. Follow me." And he led the way toward the town.

A lone guard melted back into deep shadow, his musket at his side, saying nothing as we passed into Newport.

He took me to a nearby house, the house of a well-to-do man by the look of it, smelling of fresh paint, with shutters framing the leaded-glass windows and candlelight glowing within. Following him into the sitting room, I finally had a look at the man.

He was middle-aged, a little stout—rather like my father in appearance. From beneath his periwig, his eyes twinkled with a curious look, and I thought, *Surely, this is a friend.* I felt myself relax, thanking heaven he had found me. I sat in the chair he offered and waited while he instructed a servant as to our refreshment. A fire burned in the grate. Warmth spread over me like butter on hot bread. I suddenly felt very, very tired.

In the morning, the pirates would find themselves surrounded. The nightmare was finally, finally over.

He sat across from me, a smile crinkling the corners of his eyes. "Your name?"

"Oh, sorry. Daniel Markham of Boston." Just then the servant returned, handing each of us a mug of spiced cider.

"I must say," my friend continued, taking a drink of his cider, "you've intrigued me terribly. What's a fine lad from Boston doing on a Newport wharf in the middle of the night?"

I did not answer immediately. Instead, I cupped the mug in my hands and sipped my cider. It was hot and, like the fire, seemed to melt through me. I sipped again and again. A sleepiness pressed upon me, a delicious sleepiness. I settled back in my chair, cradled my mug, and finally told my story.

I started at the beginning, with Father's marriage to Faith and our sudden move to Jamaica. I told him about the attack, the murder, Faith's illness. Halfway through my story, I even unclasped my locket and showed him my mother's likeness and told him she was the daughter of the governor and that I was the governor's grandson and that both my grandfather and my mother had died long ago. I thought he'd want to know.

He listened intently, rubbing his chin, occasionally saying, "I see," or "'Tis a shame," or "Poor, poor lad," or "Drink up, now."

As I talked, I could scarcely keep my eyes open. My tongue thickened. My words slurred together. "They've no idea I've escaped. If we surround them, they'll have nowhere to go come dawn. It will be over. Then the men who murdered my father will face the justice they deserve."

The embers snapped, sending a billow of sparks up the chimney. The man said nothing and leaned back into his chair, lost in shadow. I realized, with a heavy sleepiness, that I did not even know his name. But it did not matter. He would take care of everything now. *Besides,* I thought, *I am too sleepy. And my head is so heavy. . . .*

I heard the town crier cry, "One o'clock and all's well." I heard movement behind me.

My friend asking, "What took you so long?"

A voice replying, "Did anyone see?"

"None excepting the guard, and he'll say nothing."

A hand on my shoulder. "Come, Daniel, my boy. 'Tis time to leave." A hand under my arm, urging me to my feet. Eyes of black swimming before me like pools of midnight.

So sleepy . . .

CHAPTER
6

For days I huddled by the rail, wrapped in a blanket.

For days nothing met my gaze except an endless ocean, an endless sky. All gray, everything gray.

Of course, there was much movement around me on the fo'c'sle deck—with this many men aboard, it was impossible to be entirely alone. Men gambling, drinking, mending sails or tarring ropes if the mood struck them, playing fiddles, dancing, target shooting, or spinning raucous yarns. But I ignored the yarns, the music, the shooting, and the men. I only took the food that was offered me, shrugging off anyone who tried to pat my shoulder or talk to me.

I dreamed of Boston. I dreamed of my father and the way things used to be. And always, when my eyes would clear of my dream, there would be the ocean. The endless, gray ocean.

I cursed my life. I cursed Josiah Black. I cursed the man from Newport who had called himself my "friend." Doubtless he had mixed some sleeping potion into my cider. I scarcely remembered Josiah rowing me back to the *Tempest Galley.* "Breathe not a word about what you've done," he had whispered before I collapsed into a deep sleep.

Much as I did not want to admit that Josiah was right about anything, I knew enough to stay silent. Josiah was the only one, it appeared, who knew what I'd done, or rather, what I'd intended to do. In fact, so certain had Josiah been of my intentions, he'd earlier arranged to have his friend on the dock, waiting for me. I knew if the pirates found out I'd meant to betray them, I'd not live to catch my next breath. So I huddled by the rail, wrapped in my blanket, staring at nothing, saying nothing, cursing my miserable life.

One day as I cursed my miserable life, my memory regarding the *Norfolk* crawled back into my mind, spinning its spidery web, despite all my attempts to push it away. I remembered finding the *Norfolk*'s manifest on the night my father had announced we were moving to Jamaica. I remembered showing it to my father. Him setting it aside, brushing away my questions, saying, *I'll take care of it later . . . Daniel, please. Not now.*

I wondered, *How on earth would my father have had the manifest in his possession, unless . . . unless . . .*

Strand by strand, I untangled the web until I could no longer deny the truth.

It was so simple.

My father had known. He'd known what kind of men took supper at the family board. He'd known what kind of men hoisted me onto their shoulders. He'd known what kind of men gave me treasures—treasures stained with blood. He'd known, and he'd never told me. He'd known, and still he sat in the best pew at the meetinghouse.

A wretched despair stole over my soul just as the heavens opened and sheets of water poured from the sky. I pulled my blanket tighter and hung my head. *Why, Father, why?* Rainwater streamed off my cocked hat and puddled in my lap.

Even so, I love you.

"Hey, Daniel," someone said, "sitting out here getting soaked to the innards is no place for anybody with half a brain. Go below where it's warmer or you'll catch your death."

I pulled the blanket over my head.

"Besides," he added, "today's a celebration. It'll do you good to dance awhile and gamble a bit. I'll even show you how to play dice. And just to be fair, I'll make certain you have a bit of beginner's luck."

After yammering another minute or so, he went away, to my relief. So did most of the others, making only a halfhearted attempt to get me to join them. Then from beneath me I heard music, soft at first, growing louder as more instruments joined the song. I heard laughter, singing, and the tromp of shoes.

Below me, the waters swirled by. I watched the whorls, the bubbles, and wondered what it would feel like to jump in and have the ocean press about me. It would be vast and numbing. I imagined the ship's hull above me as I sank, watching the ship become smaller, smaller, until it finally disappeared. All around me, it would be silent. Dark. Ended.

A voice startled me. "Daniel?" It was Josiah.

Go away, I thought.

He thrust a gift under my nose. "I have something for you." It was wrapped in velvet, tied with a golden cord. "Merry Christmas."

I blinked water from my eyes. *Christmas? Is it truly Christmas?* Slowly, I reached for the package, wondering at the same time if I should really take it or if I should ignore him. Just as slowly, I untied it.

The velvet wrapping fell away.

It was a carving of a boy. Made of ivory, the figure stood about four inches tall. With a blanket draping carelessly from one hand and a thumb in his mouth, he gazed upward at something unseen. But I knew what he was looking at. I was that boy.

I remembered a night from my childhood when the fire blazed beside me. I remember gazing at Josiah while he carved, while he told me to not move a muscle, that if I was a good lad he would tell me a story. I can't remember if I was good. I can't remember the story. I remember only staring at him. His hair of jet black, tied in a queue at the back of his neck. His rough fingers as he carved and carved. His occasional smile of satisfaction. His beautiful teeth.

I set my jaw, held my hand out over the gray, swirling waters, and released the figure. It fell noiselessly into the water below and sank into vastness, into numbness, its ivory eyes watching the ship grow smaller and smaller. "My family doesn't celebrate Christmas."

He said nothing and walked away.

The next day, my time at the rail ended.

I was half asleep, wondering whether Faith had recovered from her illness or whether she was with my father in heaven, when suddenly someone ripped my blanket away. "Hey!" I cried indignantly, swinging around to see who it was.

Josiah stood there, his face twisted with fury. Before I could react, he crumpled my blanket into a ball and heaved it into the ocean. "Get up!" he shouted. When I did not move, he placed a well-aimed kick on my behind. "Get up, I say!"

I scrambled to my feet, my face flushing, aware of the slew of onlookers, most of whom were grinning.

"You have bled long enough! It is time to be a part of this crew! You must shoulder your weight, else I'll toss you overboard as useless cargo!"

I almost told him to go ahead and toss me overboard, but suddenly feared he'd do exactly as he promised. I swallowed hard and mumbled, "I don't know what to do."

He shoved me toward the foremast. "Climb aloft and keep a lookout. And, boy, whatever you do, hang tight and don't look down."

The foremast swayed above me like a massive tree with vines, moaning with the brisk wind. *Climb aloft? Keep a lookout? Up there?* "But—but what do I look out for?"

Josiah did not answer, for he had gone. Many of the men still watched me, and there was nothing for it but to do what Josiah ordered. I grasped the shrouds and began to climb, thinking angrily, *He orders me around like I am some servant and he my master. He told me a pirate captain can give orders only during chase or battle, and yet he orders me around as if I have nothing to do except whatever he says.*

Distracted by my anger, I forgot Josiah's warning and looked down. The deck lurched beneath me. Had I climbed so far already? I clung to the ratlines and closed my eyes, fighting waves of nausea and dizziness. My body began to shake violently.

Curse you, Josiah Black.

After more clinging, grasping, climbing, and cursing, I finally reached the crosstrees—the lookout station. I tied myself to the mast with my belt, wondering why Josiah thought he could trust me with such a post. Why should I alert the crew to anything? What did I care about them? If I saw a rock, I would merely brace myself. If I saw a merchant ship, I would warn it away. If I saw a man-o'-war, I would invite its crew aboard and laugh as they hanged all the villains for piracy, murder, and kidnapping.

I stayed tied to the mast for hours. Finally, in the semidarkness of evening, I climbed down, starving. I ate enough food to fill three men, drank a ladle of stale water, curled up by the rail, shivering, and fell asleep. Being a lookout was hard work.

I awakened once in the middle of the night. A blanket covered me. It smelled of wool, tobacco, and rum. I pulled it over my head, glad of the warmth, and fell asleep again.

The next day and the next found me back at the lookout post. I was beginning to enjoy it. High in the rigging, I felt a separation from the crew, as if I were no longer aboard a pirate ship and was instead in my own world, a world of endless sky and endless sea, where the events of the past few weeks seemed unreal. Like whispers in the night.

One sullen, misty day, I spied something that made my heart sink: a ship. About a half mile distant, blind to our presence, she sailed an intercept course. Unless I warned it away, it would surely suffer the same fate as the *Gray Pearl*. So far, none of the pirates had spotted it. I acted quickly, for I had a plan.

I removed my shirt, a cotton shirt that was fast becoming tattered and grayed. I tied my scarlet-colored stocking to one of the sleeves. From a distance, if I was lucky, it would look like blood. Hopefully, when the merchant ship saw the bloodstained shirt, they would realize who we were and slip away before the pirates were any the wiser.

Silently, I undid my belt. I stood at the crosstrees and waved the shirt above my head.

They saw me at the same time.

The other ship's lookout.

Josiah.

I saw the glint of a spyglass as their lookout spotted me, while at the same time I glanced below to see Josiah staring at me, agape. He strode to the forward rail and cried, "Sail two points off the leeward bow!" Immediately men scrambled to posts.

With every sail sheeted to its fullest, the *Tempest Galley* surged forward. Beneath me the pirates hid behind bulwarks and masts, crouched between cannon. I saw the glint of weapons and the loading of pistols, heard the murmur of anticipation. There was Will Putt, a brace of pistols across his chest, a cutlass in one hand, a pistol in the other, and a grin smeared across his face. There was Josiah, motionless, waiting. He glanced at me, and although his expression did not change, I knew he was angry. Fearing what he might do to me when he had the chance, fearing that his patience with me was finally at an end, I looked away.

To my dismay, the merchant ship stayed her course.

Two hundred yards . . .

One hundred . . .

Her yards swung and she loosed her sails. I saw the power go out of her as the helm was put down smartly and her fore topsail backed with the breeze.

A few men scurried about our ship as well, preparing to heave to, pretending to be merchant crewmen following the orders of a merchant captain.

The ships drew abreast.

"Do you require assistance?" cried her captain through a speaking trumpet. "We saw—"

Suddenly the pirates erupted from their hiding places, raised their weapons above their heads, and screamed.

My scalp prickled.

The merchant vessel swung her rudder, but she had no steerage way. Her crew darted this way and that—up the shrouds, down the hatches. "Brace full!" I heard her captain shout. "Sheet home! Sheet home!" Her gun ports opened.

But it was too late. Grappling lines soared from our ship like the silken strands of a spider. Musical instruments snarled like wolves, and my heart thumped with the heavy beat of the drum.

$\mathcal{L}$ike cockroaches, the pirates swarmed onto the other ship.

I clung to the mast, watching, paralyzed with terror.

As a body, the sailors of the merchant ship raised their arms in surrender, some falling to their knees, pleading for their lives.

Just then, the merchant captain—a tall, strapping, bewigged gentleman—stepped across the quarterdeck, raised his pistol, and fired at a pirate. The man screamed in agony, clutched his chest, and crumpled to the deck. I screamed too, high as I was, seeing an image of my father lying dead in a pool of blood. *No! Not again!*

At first the pirates stood unmoving, as if in shock, as if they could not believe that anyone dared oppose them. But then they flooded the quarterdeck, enraged, shouting vengeance, and the captain disappeared under the mob of cutthroats. I looked away, unwilling to watch, nevertheless seeing in my mind the blades dripping in blood.

God have mercy upon his soul, I prayed.

With the death of the captain, it was over.

I watched from above as they heaved the captain's body overboard and began to go through the ship's manifest and scour the vessel for loot. The men of the *Mercury* were invited to join the brotherhood of pirates. A few came forward. One man was forced to join, as it was discovered he was a musician and the pirates needed music. Music for dancing, they said. And music for killing—music so horrifying God himself begged for mercy.

I clung to the mast.

Throughout the rest of the day, while the *Mercury* was pillaged, I dreamed with my eyes open, staring at the horizon. I saw pirates swarm like cockroaches. A dignified merchant captain raising his firearm. Pistols belching bullet and powder. Men on their knees, begging for mercy. I squeezed my eyes shut, ignoring the calls from below for me to come down. That there was food and fresh water and a prize to be had. That they had no hard feelings because I had fallen asleep on my watch. Because I had not warned them. That little Daniel Markham was their friend. That they knew I wouldn't let it happen again. But soon they forgot me, for as night descended, the music and dancing, the games and gambling, began. Roars of drunkenness continued through the night, spluttering laughter, a fight or two, quickly broken up.

I wondered why Josiah had told his crew that I had fallen asleep on duty when both he and I knew that I had, in fact, attempted to betray the pirates a second time. I wondered why he didn't, indeed, just toss me overboard as useless cargo. Part of me wished he would, for then this nightmare would be ended. Tightening my belt around the mast, I slumped against it, unable to stop the heaviness of sleep.

The music continued, boisterous and merry.

I was dreaming of fresh bread, cider, and ham with beans when a hand clasped my ankle and yanked it roughly. Startled, I cried out.

Then, out of the darkness, an enormous, shadowy head loomed. Foul breath, rum, and armpit odor wafted over me as he snarled, "Hand over your locket, boy." I heard the rasp of steel.

The shape lunged at me, but I dodged, horrified when my belt held me in place and I could scarcely move. I felt the slice of steel in my arm, cold and terrifying. He lunged at me again. "No!" I placed one foot squarely against his chest, meanwhile frantically trying to unlatch my belt. I heard breathing, ragged and desperate, vaguely realizing it was coming from me.

"Why, you—" the man started, but he said no more as I shoved his chest with all my might. I felt him slip, heard the whisper of metal as the dagger fell. He cursed, and I hoped for a brief moment that he might follow his dagger. But even as I thought it, he grabbed my ankle and climbed up my body as if he were climbing a rope.

My leg. My pants waist. My arm. My collar.

Me, fighting and struggling.

With a snarl, he wrenched my locket from my neck, then wrapped a giant hand about my throat and squeezed. "Foolish boy! You should have just given it to me!" My eyes bulged, and I couldn't breathe. I still fumbled with my belt, kicking him weakly. I felt myself fading. *No! Father, help me!*

My belt snapped. Suddenly released, I fell. Away from the mast, away from the hand that crushed me. I screeched. I flailed through the air, reaching for something, anything.

I grazed the yard with my shoulder and bounced into the shrouds. It was like landing in a net, but a net set on its ear. I began to fall down the shrouds but grasped hold, nearly yanking my arms from their sockets. A body hurtled past me. A moment passed, no more, before there was a heavy thud below. Then came cries of surprise and an abrupt stop to the music.

The pirate—whoever he was—had fallen. From where I lay, clinging to the ratlines, I saw others gather around him, holding a lantern high.

"Dead," said one, prodding the body with his foot. "Snapped his neck like a chicken."

"Must've taken a bad step," said another. "Always was a stupid oaf. Never liked him."

"Owed me money, that one. Now he don't got to pay. Lucky bloke."

They peered into the shrouds for a moment. "Oh, well," one of them said, shrugging. "Maybe the kid did him in." Everyone laughed as if it were a grand joke, the music started up again, and the pirates returned to their games of dice, to their dancing. The body lay crumpled on the deck, forgotten.

I crept down the ratlines, my legs like jelly. I could scarcely believe what had happened. Someone had almost killed me just to get his grimy hands on my locket! These men were beasts, all of them. I strode to the corpse. I pried open his fingers and yanked back my locket.

"Animal!" I screamed, kicking him. "Now you've done it! You've broken my chain!" I kicked him again and again, knowing he couldn't feel it, wishing he could. "Lay your filthy hands on me again, and I'll—I'll—kill you! A-again!"

"Daniel." Josiah spoke from beside me, his voice silken. "Daniel, my boy, come with me." He steered me away from the body. He steered me under the quarterdeck and into his cabin. I let him steer me, for I did not care. I cared about nothing except my locket. No one, absolutely no one, was going to ever touch my locket again.

"Take this," said Josiah. To my surprise, he handed me a sleek, polished dagger. It was eight inches long or thereabouts, slender, the steel engraved with a curled design. Its sheath was of mahogany, rich and red-grained.

I took the dagger, thinking, *The next man who touches me will feel this in his ribs.*

"You're bleeding." Josiah tossed me a rag, and I pressed it to my wound. I had forgotten I was wounded. I winced, suddenly feeling the pain.

"He attacked me." My voice trembled with rage. "He had no right. He took my locket. He tried to stab me. He was strangling me. I couldn't breathe. He grabbed my locket and broke the chain. Next man who touches me gets it! I mean it! If anyone so much as . . ." I stopped talking because Josiah was looking at me strangely. "What?"

For a moment, Josiah said nothing. Then he uncorked a bottle of rum, filled two goblets, and handed one to me. "Odd how you would kill a man over a locket, don't you think, Daniel? Are we really so different?"

It was as if I'd been punched in the gut and all my air blown out. I sat staring at him, my mouth hanging open like the village dunce's. Then I hurled my goblet across the room. "We are nothing alike! My father was your friend, and I hate you!" I left the cabin, slamming the door behind me.

That night I slept in the hold, hand clamped around the hilt of my dagger. I tossed and mumbled in my sleep, seeing shadowy heads materialize in the darkness. The heads bobbed and whispered like goblins. But when I struggled awake with a gasp, there was nothing—only the taste of a nightmare in my mouth.

Throughout the night, the heads appeared. My father's—missing his jaw, trying to tell me something, his tongue flapping helplessly. Faith's—skin pasty white, eyes like boiled eggs. The minister's—pounding the pulpit, shouting, "Thou shalt not kill! Thou shalt not kill!" over and over until his skin blistered and horns popped out of his skull.

One head hovered over me. It danced goblin-like in the light of a lantern. Splotches of light streaked across its face with the motion of the ship. It stared at me, round-eyed, surprised. "Daniel?" it asked in a high, girlish voice. "Daniel?"

With the strength of a nightmare, I sprang from where I lay and pointed my dagger at its throat. "Get away from me!" I snarled.

The face took shape. Frightened mouse-gray eyes. Skin smeared with bruises. Thin lips trembling. "Don't—don't hurt me, Daniel, please! It's me. Timothy Allsworth of Boston! You know, Timothy."

*F*or me, it was simple. I was no longer alone. Surrounded by murderers, thieves, and men of monstrous, sinful nature, I had found a friend.

Timothy and I had attended the same grammar school, taught by Master Noggin. Although Timothy was a year younger, we had sat together on the same hard, backless bench, reciting from the New England primer, "In Adam's fall, we sinned all." We'd shivered in the frigid air, wishing we sat in the front row next to the stove where the smart boys sat, dreaming of the day when we were old enough to no longer attend school.

For Master Noggin had been frightful. He'd bellowed and bullied, and if we did not follow his directions (or even if we did), we could be certain his ruler would soon descend to smack the backs of our hands. Or if we were terribly stupid, or worse, if we fell asleep with our noses pressed against the primer, we could be certain to feel his switch warming our backsides.

Timothy's chance to leave school had come early. At the age of eleven, he'd shipped aboard the *Mercury* as a cabin boy, and I hadn't seen him since.

Over the next few days, after the *Tempest Galley* finally finished despoiling the *Mercury* and shoved off, sails sheeted home once again, we huddled together, Timothy and I, recounting our lives since last we'd seen the other. Sometimes we crouched beside a cannon in the waist deck. Sometimes we ran to the fo'c'sle deck, where we gazed out over the bowsprit, where the noise of sea spray drowned out our words to all but us. Sometimes when it was my turn as lookout, we climbed to the masthead, gazing at the horizon, at the bubbling white of our wake. Or sometimes we met in the hold, slipping inside an enormous coil of rope to sit with our knees butted against our chins, scarce able to wag our tongues.

It was easy to slip inside the coil with Timothy Allsworth, for he was pencil-thin. In fact, everything about Timothy was thin— his nose, his lips, his twiglike arms, even his toes, which rather looked like earthworms. But he had a monstrous head of nut-brown hair, always seeming blown by the wind.

Of course I told him everything that had happened to me. About my father, and Faith. About Josiah, Will Putt, and the man who had tried to kill me. "They're murderers, you know. All of them. They killed your captain as well. Someday I will see them hang."

"I'm glad they killed Captain Hewitt," said Timothy. "He was worse than Master Noggin."

"No one could be worse than Master Noggin."

"I tell you, 'tis true. One time Captain Hewitt smacked me in the head with a bucket, and all because I didn't answer fast enough."

"Master Noggin used to do that too."

"With a bucket?"

"Well, with a ruler, anyway. Or a book."

"Buckets hurt more. Besides, there was another time when Captain Hewitt hung a basket of grapeshot around some poor fellow's neck and tied his arms to the capstan bars until blood burst from his nose and mouth. The basket must've weighed two hundred pounds. 'Tis certain Master Noggin never did that."

"But that's horrible!"

Timothy nodded. "Aye. The fellow up and died because of it, and all because he swiped two biscuits from the larder. The next day I peeked in Captain Hewitt's log and saw that he'd recorded the fellow had died of fever."

"But such an entry was a lie!"

"Aye. But Captain Hewitt, he was like a king with his own country. Once he flogged a sailor so hard his skin flayed off. Then he ordered him soaked in a barrel of brine. Then once when I was sleeping, Captain Hewitt punched me for no reason, and then because I was protecting myself, he grabbed a marlinspike and beat me with it. I still have lumps."

He pulled up his shirt, and I touched the knots of rib bone, my mouth agape.

"'Twas a torture ship," he added. "'Twas a lucky day when the pirates came to save us."

I shook my head in disbelief, running my fingers over the skin on his back, over welted scars from whippings, like the tangled branches of a tree, wondering.

"You see, Daniel," he whispered, "I'll take freedom over torture any day."

Was that why so many men willingly turned pirate? Was it more than just a thirst for blood or riches? Even to think such a thought seemed a betrayal of my father. And yet for the first time, I admit, I was uncertain of the answer.

A few days later as Timothy's bruises faded to yellow and green, I found him on the fo'c'sle deck, scrubbing out his laundry in a wooden tub, the tangy smell of soap sharp in the air. He sang, his voice like a Sabbath angel, soap suds up to his elbow. Over our heads, freshly laundered clothes hung from the rigging, flapping in the stiff breeze. Droplets spattered. A damp sleeve brushed across my face.

"That's a lot of laundry," I said.

Timothy grinned. "Some of the fellows are paying me to wash their clothes. I really need the money, seeing as I'm not going to get paid for my two years aboard the *Mercury* and my mother's counting on me to bring something home. For all I know, she's in the poorhouse by now."

His mother. Poor lady. I remembered the Widow Allsworth well—frail, bent, drenching a dozen handkerchiefs on the day her only son left for sea. I imagined her sitting alone in her house, waiting and waiting for Timothy to return, not knowing what had happened to him. I chewed my lip, wondering if I should tell Timothy that it was blood money he was earning.

"Need your clothes washed?" he asked, giving my clothing a close scrutiny. "I'll do it for free."

I glanced down at myself. My clothes were grayed, rumpled, and beginning to look downright ragged. My trunk of nice clothing, which I'd taken with me from Boston, now lay at the bottom of the ocean. I was wearing all I owned—a pathetic wardrobe for the grandson of a governor. I sighed and looked away. "No."

Timothy stood, soapy water sliding off his arms. "Look,

Daniel, if you're going to be sailing all the way to the Red Sea, you'll need more than just one set of clothes. Here, take these." And, selecting from a pile beside him, he handed me several shirts, pants, vests, stockings, and drawers.

"But—"

"Don't worry. They don't belong to anyone here."

I frowned. "What do you mean, they don't belong to anyone here? Then where did they—" my voice caught. "They're Captain Hewitt's, aren't they?"

Timothy went back to scrubbing the clothes in the tub. Water splashed out on my shoe, trickling between my toes. Finally he said, "My mother used to say that when life gives you a bees' nest, look for the honey."

When still I hesitated, Timothy urged, "Go on, take them. Captain Hewitt certainly doesn't need them anymore. Consider it my pay for two years of working for the tyrant. Besides, come a month or so, you won't be so picky when all you're wearing is a thread or two."

I fingered the clothing. They were fine shirts, linen, stitched with skill. And the breeches—as first-rate as my father's. They would be a little big, but it was better than wearing rags. Plus, I felt sure that Captain Hewitt, could he speak to me now, would *want* me to have them, seeing as I was a hostage at the hands of the very men who had murdered him and would someday see all his murderers hang for their crimes. "Thanks, Timothy."

"Don't mention it. Now get out of those god-awful stinky clothes and hand them over before I retch into the washtub."

The cutlass sliced toward my head. I parried, grunting, my arm trembling with fatigue. Steel clashed and scraped.

Still he came at me, again and again, his face black as cinder, his lips stretched in a grin so wide that his teeth shone like a skeleton's.

He was well muscled and lithe, bald as a cannonball, with a laugh that sounded both cruel and contented. I yelled as I lunged, thrusting the cutlass toward his chest, but with a quick flick of his wrist, he parried and sidestepped, tripping me with his foot.

I fell onto the sand, rolling at the same time. But before I could gain my feet, the point of his cutlass was at my throat. I dropped my weapon and lay motionless. A pinprick of pain jabbed my Adam's apple.

"You dead, Fat Boy," said Caesar, still grinning. "I win again."

He removed his cutlass, and I sat up, wincing, rubbing my throat. "Do you have to make it so real?"

Caesar shrugged. "This way you not be surprised when it battle. You be tough. Don't forget to beat my sword back before you try for kill. That why you lose."

"Is it my turn yet?" asked Timothy. He sat under a palm tree, chewing his fingernails. The wind made his hair look wild as Cook's mop.

About a month ago, Josiah had asked Caesar to teach both Timothy and me swordsmanship—trying to turn me into one of them, no doubt. Caesar, who seemed to like nothing better than slashing, tearing, ripping, stabbing, and all manner of destruction aimed at the flesh, readily agreed. Now Caesar crouched, cutlass slicing through the air. A slow grin spread across his face, and he motioned Timothy toward him. "Come get me, Choirboy."

As Timothy and Caesar crossed swords, I flopped beneath the palm. We were anchored at a deserted island off the west coast of Africa. As soon as the pirates finished lazing about and filling up the water casks, we planned to head southwest, catch the westerlies, and sail around Africa's Cape of Good Hope into the Indian Ocean.

I squeezed a handful of sand, then watched it trickle from between my fingers. Caesar didn't know this, but I was learning swordsmanship only so that I could defend myself against the likes of him. Never would I raise my sword against another in battle. Never. (Even Timothy didn't know this, because now he was one of them. The day before, he'd participated in pillaging one of the villages on another island. I'd watched in horror from the rail while he'd helped load pigs, chickens, goats, turtles, and fruit into the longboat. *Thief! What would your poor mother say?*)

"You'll be glad of it when we're months out at sea," Timothy had said in answer to my accusing stare once he climbed back aboard. "Even pirates can starve. You should try it sometime. Maybe then you won't be so high and mighty."

Now I threw a fistful of sand, cursing when it caught the wind and blasted back into my eyes. *Thief or not,* I thought, crying into my sleeve, *Timothy's my only friend.*

I didn't notice they had approached until I saw their feet out of the corner of my gritty eye. Nine of them—feet, that is. Plus one wooden stump. Some feet were shod in leather boots, some in square-toed shoes; others were bare. One foot had only two toes. I glanced up, blinking.

Five men stood facing me, including Josiah, his face expressionless. Basil Higgins, the quartermaster for the *Tempest Galley,* a fair and decent fellow as far as murderers went, held a parchment. Manuel Featherstone, the scar-eyed man, short and wiry and deadly with a dagger, held a pot of ink and a quill. Will Putt clutched a Bible. Then there was one-legged Abe Corner, who'd run away at age twelve and was now the company cook. Beside Abe was a barrel.

"Daniel Markham?" Basil had a crooked nose—smashed in battle, no doubt—and eyebrows so bushy they grew together in the middle. A mat of curly hair peeped out from behind the brace of pistols strapped across his chest. I remembered him from when I was a child and liked him.

"Aye."

"We've business to discuss with ye."

It seemed to me that everything became instantly quiet. The clash of swords ceased. Even the birds stopped squawking and twittering.

"You've been with us three months now—"

"Two."

Basil cleared his throat, his voice deep and raspy, as though he'd been hacked across the neck too many times. "The point being, young Daniel, we don't allow no one aboard who won't sign the Articles." He held out the parchment. Written across the parchment were a dozen paragraphs or so. At the bottom were numerous signatures, scrawled in halting form, X's scratched everywhere.

My mouth fell open. Surely they weren't serious! "But—but you took me against my will!"

"Aye, that may be true, but you're one of us now."

"I'll *never* be one of you!" I looked from face to face, my temples throbbing. "You murdered my father! You're all devils!"

They stared at me. Then Basil shrugged. "Very well, lad. Have it your way." He withdrew a pistol and laid it at my feet.

"What's that for?" I asked.

Basil didn't answer.

Abe Corner tapped the cask beside him with his peg leg. "Full of sailor's biscuit. Water's about a hundred paces that way." He pointed over his shoulder.

Biscuit? Water? A pistol? Do they plan to leave me here?

As if to answer my question, they began to walk away. Caesar and Timothy followed them. Timothy glanced back. "Farewell, Daniel."

My heart began a horrible pounding, and my ears roared with blood. I ran after them, grabbing Josiah's sleeve. "Josiah, you can't be serious!"

Josiah turned, his face hard. "The Articles are for the benefit of all the men, including yourself. Rules keep things fair and everyone honest." He stared at me unblinking before looking away. His voice softened. "They took a vote, Daniel, my boy. I'm sorry, but if you don't sign the Articles, you have to stay behind."

I snorted. "You talk of honesty? You, a pirate and a murderer?"

Josiah hesitated, and in that moment I glimpsed pity in the depths of his black eyes. Pity, and . . . something else. "I'm sure you'll make the right decision." He pried his sleeve out of my fist, turned, and walked off with the others.

"But—but you can't leave me. I—I'm your hostage!" The wind gusted. Sand peppered my legs. My hair whipped into my eyes. I glanced about me. A sandy beach. A few palms, scrubby trees, and grasses. A mountain in the center of the island—a volcano, probably, like the one we'd seen smoking just a few leagues away. With just a pistol and a cask of biscuit, I wouldn't last long. And no one, other than Timothy and this band of cutthroats, even knew I was here.

They reached the longboat, climbed inside, and set their oars to the locks.

They're leaving me. They're actually leaving me!

And with a creak of the oarlocks, they shoved off as the last man climbed aboard.

They can't leave me! They can't! I'll die! "No! No!" I shrieked, running into the water. The oars stopped. Seven faces stared at me. Stumbling, water lapping about my thighs, I reached the boat and grabbed the gunwale. "Don't leave! I'll sign."

Basil nodded, cleared his throat, and read the Articles, paragraph by paragraph.

Every man to have a vote in affairs. Food and drink to be divided equally. . . .

All prizes to be divided equally. Captain and quartermaster to get double shares. If a man robs the company, his ears and nose will be slit, and he will be marooned on a sandbar. . . .

If anyone loses a limb, he will be given eight hundred dollars. Three hundred dollars for an eye.

Cowardice or deserting the ship in battle is punishable by death.

All men must keep pistols and cutlasses clean and ready for service. . . .

My vision blurred. My throat swelled. I placed my hand on the Bible.

My voice sounded far away. "I, Daniel Markham, swear an oath on the Bible to abide by these Articles."

A quill was thrust into my hand, the parchment placed over the Bible. I heard the scratch of my signing, feather against paper. A splotch of ink spread across the parchment like blood.

They hauled me aboard and I sat, my heart dry as sand, ignoring Timothy, who patted me on the back, saying that he was glad I had come to my senses. That it was all for the best. That forced men couldn't be condemned for piracy, so I was safe no matter what happened.

I looked out over the harbor to where the *Tempest Galley* lay anchored.

It was unthinkable that I would lie while taking an oath upon the Bible. Such profaning of holy things would damn my soul to eternal torment in the lake of fire and brimstone.

Aye, I will abide by your miserable Articles, Josiah Black, I told myself. *But I am not a pirate. I am not a thief. I am not a murderer. And never will I be.*

Then a wretchedness from deep within burst out like pus from a wound. Hot. Scathing. I hid my face on my knees and sobbed.

Late that night, as men danced to the raucous music blasting from the fo'c'sle deck, I sat between two cannon, cross-legged, a lantern beside me. Upon my request, Basil Higgins had given me a parchment, a bottle of ink, and a quill.

To Whom It May Concern,
I am a forced man. I have signed the Articles of the Tempest Galley

by force, not by choice. I am not a pirate, nor a thief, nor a murderer.
I am a hostage.

It was not perfect. Master Noggin would no doubt toss it in the stove and tell me to write it over, this time with straight lines and without ink splotches. But it was good enough for my purposes, and besides, Master Noggin was far away.

As I signed my name, Timothy approached, carrying a platter heaped with roasted chicken and yams. He settled beside me, the lantern between us. "What are you doing?"

Though I was still angry at him, I showed him the paper.

"Blood and thunder, that's messy. Master Noggin's probably having apoplexy right now."

"It's for the courts. In case we get captured." I read it aloud while he chewed on a drumstick, his chin glistening with grease.

"Chicken?" he asked when I was done, offering me the platter. "Abe gave me extra so you could have some. He said you haven't eaten all day."

I almost said no, remembering where the chicken and yams had come from, remembering that Timothy was a thief, but my stomach hurt and the smell was like heaven. I took a piece. "I'll need a couple of witnesses," I was saying, my mouth full. Grease dripped onto the parchment.

"Sure, I'll sign." Wiping his hand on his shirt, Timothy took up the quill, dipped it in ink, and signed his name followed by the word *wittnes*. "Daniel, just so you know, I knew that you'd sign the Articles. We all did."

I was silent.

"That's one reason why we all voted to maroon you. Because we knew you'd sign."

"Even Josiah?"

"No, not him. He was the only one who voted otherwise."

I chewed my chicken, surprised, digesting this bit of information, wondering why Josiah would vote on my behalf, why he had not thrown me overboard a dozen times already. Perhaps it was because I was too valuable a hostage—after all, I *was* the grandson of the former governor. "I need another signature. Maybe Caesar will be a witness too."

Timothy frowned. "He can't."

"Why not?"

"Because slaves can't be witnesses."

My mouth dropped open in shock. A piece of chicken plopped onto the parchment before I closed my mouth and swallowed. "Caesar's a *slave*?"

"Used to be, anyway. Him and Cicero and Tom and August. All of them. Here they receive equal treatment. They've signed the Articles just like everyone else."

It was difficult to fathom . . . slaves receiving equal treatment. I didn't know what to make of it, only knowing that, despite myself, I liked Caesar. Before my lesson just that morning he had given me a gift of a crossbelt and cutlass, saying it was time Fat Boy stopped using his.

"I'd rather be one of the Brethren any day than a slave," Timothy added.

"Maybe Abe Corner will sign my statement, then."

"Abe's a good choice." Timothy wiped his hands on his shirt. "Well, the music's calling me. I'm going to go dance. Want to come?"

"My father says dancing is of the devil."

Timothy sighed and shrugged. "I dunno, Daniel, but it seems like hell's a much livelier place. There's rum and brandy in case you change your mind."

As Timothy left, I leaned against the cannon. The fiddle began a melancholy tune, its notes soaring, soaring, seeming to reach the stars above. A guitar played alongside, plaintive notes plucked from each string. It was fine music. Even my father would agree. I closed my eyes and let the music wash over me, absently wondering whether I'd rather be a pirate or a slave.

Much as I hated to admit it, Josiah Black navigated a ship as well as any merchant captain. Just four months after leaving the New World, surviving storms and raging seas, her hull battered and her sails ragged, the *Tempest Galley* hove to in the bay of Saint Mary's, a lushly green, low-lying island off the eastern coast of Madagascar.

The April day was warm and breezy, the sands white like sugar, the water blue as turquoise.

Two ships lay at anchor—the *Defiance* and the *Sweet Jamaica*. Aye, pirate ships they were, for Saint Mary's was a pirates' nest. Before we even dropped anchor, dozens of villains swarmed into longboats and rowed out to greet us. They climbed aboard, and soon the *Tempest Galley* teemed with pistol blasts, laughter, vile language, and the clink of bottles.

"Hey, Daniel!" Timothy was on the fo'c'sle deck, lounging around a bowl of rum punch with several others. I could tell by the slur in his voice that he was already half seas over. "C'mon. This stuff'll set your throat afire and send your stomach to hell." And so saying, he belched juicily and collapsed into gales of laughter as men thumped him on the back.

I tried to smile but was, once again, sorely disappointed in Timothy. No matter how many times I had warned him of the eternal consequences of such riotous living, Timothy had nevertheless thrown in his lot with the devil and embraced the life of sin with gleeful abandon. He didn't seem to care anymore that they had murdered my father, even saying once that my father was no more innocent than were the pirates, and that I had to wake up and smell the stink.

Now I replied, "No, thanks. Not thirsty."

"Thinks he's too good for us, does he?" one of the pirates mumbled. A greasy mustache drooped over his lip, and his darting eyes reminded me of a rat's.

I looked toward shore, pretending I couldn't hear, wishing these ruffians weren't swarming all over our ship as if they owned it.

"Ah, never mind him," said Timothy. "He's always like that."

"Aye, well, that may be so," the pirate replied. "Can't say I recommend it, though, as a way of living. I once knew a man who was high-and-mighty like that. Hated everything and everyone. So I slit his throat and fed his innards to my dog."

As everyone started to laugh, Timothy included, a pistol blasted from beside me. Startled, ears ringing, I turned to see Josiah Black glaring at the man who had just spoken. Smoke hovered above Josiah's head. "And I knew a man," said Josiah, smiling slowly, "who drowned in his own blood because he didn't treat his dog with respect."

The man paled. His mustache twitched. "Cap-Captain Black! I—I didn't know this was your ship. I—I didn't know you was back on the Round. Honest." He flicked his gaze over me. "And I was just pulling his leg. Having a bit of fun. Honest I was."

"That's right," slurred Timothy, swaying back and forth. "Rat Eye was just pulling his fun and having a bit of leg."

Josiah sighed, stuck his pistol back in his sash, and pulled me away. I shrugged out of his grasp. "Daniel, my boy, it's best you act as if you're one of them," he said softly. "Aboard my ship, I can protect you, but acting superior around men like these will only get you killed. They've had their fill of superiority."

I said nothing, wondering why he was talking to me, again wondering why, after thousands of miles, he continued to show me kindness and protect me. Did he not care that I hated him?

"Why don't you go get yourself something to eat? Surely you're as heartily sick of salt beef and wormy biscuit as I am. There's pineapple, coconut, and yams, and Cook's roasting some pigs. Go ashore if you like."

I frowned. "But what will I do ashore?"

"It's paradise, Daniel. I'm sure you'll figure it out."

"Why, blast my hide," someone exclaimed from behind us, "if it isn't that lousy scoundrel Josiah Black!"

Josiah turned and smiled. "Gideon Fist! Thought someone would have stabbed you in the back by now!"

With a black kerchief around his head, hoop earrings, and teeth that flashed gold, Gideon Fist was a brutish giant of a man. A massive red beard curled to his chest. When he clasped Josiah in a bear hug, pistols and cutlass clanking, I smelled a powerful waft of body odor. "*Captain* Fist to you, you dog. Captain of the *Defiance* now."

"The *Defiance*!"

"Aye."

"A fine ship, she is."

Captain Fist nodded, then fixed his gaze on me. "Who's the puppy?"

"This is my—" Josiah paused. "This is Daniel Markham. He's sharpening his teeth on our—"

"I am not a pirate," I declared, daring to look Captain Fist in the eye.

Fist's eyes narrowed, but he patted me on the back. "Of course not, lad. Of course not. I like your way of thinking. Like Robin Hood's merry men we are, taking from the rich and giving to the poor, namely, us. Nothing piratical about that. Now run along and let me and Captain Black discuss the finer points of life."

"Daniel," Josiah said when I turned to leave, "take this." He pulled one of his pistols from his sash and handed it to me. It was a fine pistol, with a handle of mahogany and swirls about its stock. "If anyone troubles you, shoot him."

CHAPTER 10

I wandered down the beach, shoes off, sand hot and soft between my toes. My stomach bulged from roasted pork and yams, and I gnawed a slice of pineapple. The tangy, sweet taste burst through my mouth like nothing I'd eaten before. Juice dribbled down my arm, down my chin.

Scattered around the beach, knots of pirates yarned, drank, and ate. Malagasy men and women, their skin tones ranging from light brown to almost black, dressed in colorful clothes, sat with them, laughing, smiling. I smelled fire smoke, tobacco, coconut, roasted fish and chicken. Children ran and played, giggling and shrieking.

Some of the pirates reclined on the verandas of their bamboo huts. Built on stilts, many of the huts were only big enough to house a pirate or two, while other huts had several rooms and were decorated with shells and flowering vines. I glimpsed furniture inside.

Abe Corner, the one-legged cook, had told me that scores of pirates lived here. They refused to go home to the cold and control of the colonies. They raided the ships in the Red Sea while the monsoon winds were favorable, then returned to their base at Saint Mary's to live with their Malagasy wives and beget their Malagasy children. One of the pirates had even built a couple of log forts, complete with cannon, to protect his life of robbery and murder.

I remembered Josiah's words to the crew when we'd first sighted Saint Mary's. "As agreed upon, every man is to give two full days of labor to the careening of the *Tempest Galley* and bending new sails to the yards. We'll rest here awhile, reprovision, and then, when the southwest monsoon begins to blow and the winds favor us, we voyage to the Red Sea." Then Josiah had drawn his cutlass. "If a man can be hanged for stealing a shilling, he might as well be hanged for stealing a fortune! What do you say, men?"

"Aye, Captain Black!" the crew had shouted. "A gold chain or a wooden leg, we'll stand by you!"

I tossed the pineapple rind into the surf and rinsed my hands. Then I continued down the beach until the sounds of merriment faded away and I heard nothing but the songs of birds, the breezy rustle of palm leaves, and the brush of water against the shore. My turn for careening the ship wasn't for two days. Until then, I was free as a whistle.

First I threw sticks into the water, as far as I could. Then I gathered a pile of shells, listening to the ocean roar inside the big ones. Next I practiced with my cutlass, hearing it sing as I sliced this way and that. I stabbed a tree trunk, again and again. I imagined a great battle, me the naval commander whom no one could slay, Timothy beside me as my second in command.

I took out my pistol and pretended to shoot the swarming pirates—rogues, every one. Hundreds of them. Timothy and I fighting back to back, protecting each other from villains coming at us from every side. Abe Corner choosing at the last moment to join our ranks, using his wooden leg with lethal effect. Basil Higgins deciding to forgo his life of plunder and so fighting alongside Abe. Caesar, unwilling to kill his favorite pupils, turning his blade upon the bloodthirsty pirates . . . By this time, I was hot and out of breath. I tied my sash around my head, wondering if I looked as mean as Gideon Fist. No longer a puppy, but a man. After all, I was fifteen plus two months now. I shrugged out of my vest and shirt, proud of the way my muscles were shaping up. I flexed and grinned. *Try to get me,* I thought.

As the afternoon sun became an orange ball, floating above the horizon, I collapsed on the sand and stared at the sky, at the sea birds floating in the breeze. The more I stared, the more a lump grew in my throat.

Timothy's voice echoed in my mind: *Your father was no more innocent than were the pirates. Wake up and smell the stink.*

But that's different! I had argued. *My father was a good man. A decent man who never harmed a living soul.*

No one's saying he wasn't decent, Timothy had replied, picking his toes as he sat atop a barrel. *I'm only saying he wasn't a saint, is all. None of us is.*

As I lay on the beach, I tried to imagine my father looking down upon me from heaven, tried to envision his face, but it kept slipping away, a vague shadow. *Can you see me, Father? Do you know where I am and what has happened to me? Do you care what is to become of me? Are you—are you in heaven?*

As daylight dimmed, I wiped my eyes and sat up, only then

noticing a trail that snaked into the jungle almost imperceptibly. An animal trail? Knowing I had only moments before night fell, I hurried down the trail, curious, pushing away vines and leaves. It was darker in the jungle, night almost. It smelled of rot, of things growing, of dampness. Three hundred paces from the beach, the path opened into a sandy clearing. Dim light filtered into the clearing from an opening overhead. An animal scuttled away into the brush.

Off to the side of the clearing stood a hut, roof long gone, elevated floor littered with jungle debris, steps broken, stinking of animal droppings. It had been a long time since anyone had lived there. I gave the floor a shake. Still solid.

Well, I thought, *what do you know. A hideaway. Secret and alone.* After pondering another moment or two, I smiled, then turned and dashed through the jungle toward the beach as if I had wings, thinking, *I claim this hut for Daniel Markham, gentleman adventurer and seeker of revenge.*

Over the next week, besides my two days spent careening the *Tempest Galley,* I worked on my hut.

First I hacked away the vines and plants that had grown over it, swept out the debris, and scrubbed both the floor and walls with vinegar to rid it of the stench. (I was delighted to learn that the floor was fine and smooth, made of some kind of hardwood.) Next I constructed rafters of bamboo like I'd seen on the other huts of the island, securing the ends with vine. Afterward I covered the rafters with banana leaves, weaving them together with more vine so they wouldn't blow off.

Both the roof and floor of the hut continued past the front wall, creating a covered veranda that, in my opinion, was quite cheery. I built railings of bamboo and fixed the rickety steps that led off the veranda to the clearing. Finally I cleaned underneath the hut and around the clearing itself. Brush, leaves, animal droppings, discarded construction materials—I hauled it all to a nearby area in the jungle that I had designated as both my privy and my dump.

I fetched my belongings from the *Tempest Galley* and brought Timothy back with me as my first houseguest. We sat on the veranda as the heavens opened and it began to rain. We chewed on pineapple slices, quite dry as rain pounded the roof of banana leaves and rivulets of water streamed off the edges. A lizard crawled along the railing. I slapped a bug on my neck, leaving a sticky smear of pineapple juice.

"Nice place," Timothy said as he gazed around, his mouth full of pineapple.

"You could move in with me."

He shrugged. "Maybe."

"There's enough room for several hammocks. Maybe Abe is looking for a place to stay. . . ." My voice trailed off as I remembered Abe was a pirate. But, I reminded myself, he was really a cook more than a pirate. In fact, it had been *years* since he'd participated in battle.

"I dunno," Timothy said.

"But I thought you liked it."

"Sure I do." Then he looked at me from beneath his mop of hair. "It's just that—you know."

"What."

He shrugged again. "Well, it doesn't seem as much fun, is all."

"Oh," I said, trying to hide my disappointment. "Tomorrow after our sword-fighting lesson with Caesar, we can build some furniture. A table and a chair, certainly. Maybe a real bed. You can sleep in it first."

He wiped his hands on his breeches. "You don't have any rum punch by any chance, do you?"

"No."

After a while, Timothy stood. "Well, I guess I'll be going."

"But—it's raining. You'll get wet. Why don't you stay here for the night? You can have the hammock."

He gave a crooked smile. "Another time. See you." And with a wave, off he ran into the hard rain, disappearing from sight down the path.

I watched the lizard for a long time, telling myself that it didn't matter.

It was still raining hours later when I blew out my candle and climbed in my hammock, the darkness of the jungle closing about me.

Sometime during the night, after the rain had stopped, I was awakened by a noise. I raised my head, listening. There it was again. Branches snapping. Leaves being thrust aside. Footsteps.

Timothy? Is that you?

I jerked up too quickly and accidentally tumbled out of my hammock. I stood, cursing, tangling my hand in my hammock, bumping my head against the wall, kicking a shoe across the floor.

Voices.

Shaking, still blurry from sleep, I lurched out onto the veranda.

Not forty paces away, three men moved toward me, following the path. One held a lantern, its brownish light casting monstrous, swaying shadows.

As yet, no one had seen me.

I returned to my hut, blindly searching for my pistol and cutlass. My hand touched the pistol, and I shoved it in the waistband of my pants, feeling the sting of metal. After groping around for a few more seconds, I touched leather—my crossbelt. I fastened on my crossbelt with its cutlass and stumbled for the door.

Without a sound, I descended the stairs and fled. A few moments later, I was at my dump. I crouched behind a plant with dense foliage, watching, breathing like a hurricane, my heart crashing, leaves wet against my cheek. Whatever these riffraff were up to, it was no good, of that I was certain. I hoped against hope they would not find my hut.

As they stepped into the clearing, I recognized two of the pirates: Rat Eye and Gideon Fist. The other pirate I did not know. Black hair sprouted from him like on an ape I had once seen in a cage back in Boston. Like the other two, he was heavily armed.

"Under the marked tree," said Fist, pointing.

"Aye," growled Rat Eye. "I remember it well."

Carved into the trunk of one of the palm trees was a crooked X. I had seen the mark before and wondered about its significance. I had a dread that I was about to find out.

Rat Eye set down the lantern, and the hairy pirate handed him a shovel before taking another shovel in hand and starting to dig. The two of them labored while Fist lit his pipe, squinting at the proceedings through the smoke. Occasionally he glanced back down the trail as if to be sure no one had followed them.

For the next half hour or so, I heard nothing but grunts and oaths, the slice of the shovels, the whisper of thrown sand, and the patter of rainwater from a jungle so recently drenched. A bug bit my arm, and I crushed the insect, hoping that whatever the scoundrels were looking for, they would find it quickly and leave. As yet, no one had tossed so much as a glance at the hut, hidden in shadows on the far side of the clearing.

Thunk! Thunk!

"Found it!" cried the hairy man.

"A lovelier sound I've never heard," said Rat Eye, grinning. He straightened, puffing hard, his shoulders and head extending above the pit. He wiped his brow with his sleeve.

"Well done, men." Fist emptied his pipe before stowing it back in his pocket. "Just set it up here next to me, and I'll take care of the rest."

With a grunt and a heave-ho, Rat Eye and Hairy hoisted a wooden chest onto the ground next to the pit. Then they clambered out of the pit as Fist took a key from around his neck, unlocked the chest, and lifted the lid. Sand trickled away, and the hinges creaked.

My breath caught. Jewels, coins, gold and silver bars, crowns, bracelets, necklaces—it was a king's ransom. Fist dug in a hand, and I heard the sound of treasure.

Rat Eye giggled, and his eyes gleamed.

Hairy grabbed a handful of loot and began to dance about. "By the devil, 'tis good to see it again. We're rich! We're bloody rich!"

"Those half-wits aboard the *Defiance* don't know we stole 'em blind," said Rat Eye. "They still think we nabbed nothing but sails and kettles aboard our last prize."

"Nor will they ever know." So saying, Fist drew two pistols, one in each hand, and aimed them at Rat Eye and Hairy.

CHAPTER
II

airy stopped midtwirl, mouth hanging. A ruby slipped from his hand.

"Cap-Captain Fist," stammered Rat Eye. "What—what're you doing?"

"I'm obliged to you rascals on three accounts," said Fist. "First, for stealing the goods. Second, for keeping your mouths shut about it. . . ."

Suddenly one of the pistols blasted. With no more than a wheeze, eyes wide, Hairy crumpled to the ground. I clamped my hand over my mouth to keep from screaming.

"And third, I'm much obliged to you for digging your grave and saving me the trouble."

Rat Eye sprang to his feet and sprinted for the jungle. He took four steps, five, before the other pistol rang out. His cry cut off, Rat Eye sprawled on his face, twitched, then lay still.

Smoke hovered about Fist's head. "Fools," he hissed. "Let what is buried stay buried."

After stowing his pistols and glancing again down the path, he pried Hairy's hand open and retrieved every diamond ring, pearl necklace, gold coin, ruby, and emerald, tossing them back into the chest. He then shoved Hairy with his booted foot. Eyes open and glazed, Hairy slid over the edge of the pit and disappeared. Fist dragged Rat Eye across the sand and flung him in after Hairy. There was a soft, sickening thud.

For a long time, Fist stood at the edge of the pit, staring down. He filled his pipe, lit it, and smoked. Soon the air reeked of tobacco. I wanted to run away as fast as I could, shrieking at the top of my lungs. The desire pushed against my breastbone, and I clenched my jaw. *Why doesn't he hurry?*

Still Fist smoked, until finally he emptied his pipe and stowed it, then bent and closed the chest. The lock clicked. He pushed the chest until it rested at the lip of the pit. With a grunt, he jumped into the hole and lifted the treasure down.

He will fill the pit, and then he will leave, I thought, wondering how long I could keep my wits together. Not only did I want to shriek bloody hell, but the damp jungle had soaked me through, insects kept biting me, my legs cramped, and slimy and sucking things crawled over my bare feet.

Fist climbed out and surveyed the situation, scratching his beard absently, as if, again, he had all the time in the world. Then, to my anguish, he took out his pipe again and strolled over to the hut. He arranged his cutlass and pistols, then sat on the top step to smoke.

By the devil! That's Fist's hut!

I almost groaned in agony, thinking of all the hours I'd spent rebuilding the place and cleaning it up. Now I realized all the time had been wasted. I couldn't stay there. Then the hair prickled on the back of my neck. Slowly, at first, then rising like a bristle brush.

My shoes are inside. My candles and tinderbox. My dagger. My hammock. A Bible. If Fist looks inside . . .

As if reading my thoughts, Fist's head jerked up, like an animal that catches a scent. He reached out and grasped the new veranda railings as if seeing them for the first time. He looked at the steps, newly repaired. Faster than I thought a giant of a man could move, he fetched the lantern from near the pit and then thundered up the steps and into the hut. I saw light gleaming and moving from between the cracks. Returning to the veranda, Fist set down the lantern and drew his cutlass.

With the rasp of steel, chills swept down my spine. Every hair on my body stood on end. *Should I run? Should I stay where I am? Should I just shoot him with my pistol? What if I miss? O God in heaven, I'm a dead man.*

Fist circled the perimeter of the clearing, quietly, slowly, brushing aside the vegetation with his cutlass and peering beyond. While there wasn't a path between the clearing and the dump where I now crouched, there must have been some kind of indication that I had passed through there, for upon reaching that point, Fist paused, knelt, and studied the ground. Then, to my horror, he stood, brushed aside vines and branches, and entered.

My God, he's coming!

I waited a few more seconds to be certain, then fled in the opposite direction, into the pitch black, my legs screaming with cramps, my ears thundering with the beat of my heart. An instant later, I stumbled over the debris pile. A sound escaped my lips. Before I even knew what I was doing, I was off and running again, blinded by the dark. I heard the crash of underbrush. Wet leaves slapped my face. I heard a curse and the sound of some-one falling, and knew Fist had likewise tumbled over the debris. Then the sounds of running. Of a cutlass slashing. And slashing. Of breathing. Heavy. Ferocious. Closer . . . *closer . . .*

Right behind me!

I whirled and drew my cutlass, whipping it through the dark-ness, hoping it would bite flesh, instead hearing the crash of metal as it met Fist's cutlass. The shock echoed up my arm. Without waiting I slashed again, missed, moving backward, stumbling over roots. Fist grunted as he swung his cutlass. I ducked, hearing the whistle of air as it passed overhead. Imme-diately I swung again, feeling my blade cut deep, hearing the *chunk* of metal on flesh and bone. Fist roared with pain.

I turned and ran, I don't know where.

It seemed I ran forever, my lungs burning, my feet cut, stum-bling, when I finally burst out of the jungle into the clearing. The lantern still sat on the veranda. Footprints and blood marred the sand. Blood turned black.

I stood for a moment, panting, dazed, then wiped my cutlass on my breeches, sheathed it, and crossed the clearing to the hut. Inside, I stuffed my belongings into my hammock, untied my hammock from its pegs, and rolled it into a bundle. I glanced around quickly and stepped back out onto the veranda.

There beside the pit, blocking the jungle trail, stood Fist. His left arm dangled limply. Blood soaked the sleeve, and I saw a gleam of bone through the gash in his clothing. In his good hand, he gripped his cutlass. And while I stood there, knowing my life was over, he grinned, his teeth glinting gold in the lantern light.

CHAPTER
12

I dropped my bundle and drew my cutlass.

It felt like hours, but it took only seconds for me to charge across the clearing. I realized my mouth was open and I was screaming. Wild-sounding, like a savage.

His eyes blazed as our cutlasses collided. He drew back his cutlass and slashed at me. I parried, thrust, and tried to whirl out of the way as his cutlass sliced my ear. Blood seeped down my neck.

Our blades crashed together again, me still screaming, screaming . . .

Then we were apart, circling, panting.

"Why don't you put down your cutlass, my lad?" Fist was saying. "No reason we can't share the treasure, is there? We'll be friends. Why shed more blood? It makes such a mess. It's already soiled your fine shirt."

"I've seen how you treat your friends, you devil."

"Have you now? Well, my hearty, that's good to know." Fast as lightning, Fist struck a blow that sent me sprawling, my cutlass flying out of my grasp.

And in the split second before he stabbed me, while the murderous light shone from his eyes, I drew my pistol, cocked it, and fired.

In a blast of smoke, Fist flew back and disappeared into the pit.

I crawled to the edge and peered over, half expecting Fist to stab me in the throat. But he lay on his back, eyes closed, his cutlass fallen from his hand. A circle of blood spread on the belly of his tunic. The air stank of blood, feces, and body odor.

It's over. My God, it's over.

I lay back and closed my eyes, tears coursing down the sides of my face into my hair, muscles quivering like jelly. I sobbed a long time, hardly believing that I had drawn my cutlass and charged Fist, hardly believing that I had crossed swords with a pirate captain and won. Of course, I'd had to win by using my pistol, but where was Fist's honor when he'd blasted his two friends into hell? *It may not have been the most honorable thing to do,* I thought, *but I am alive.*

Finally, satisfied that I'd had no other choice, not if I wished to live, I dragged myself to my feet and gathered my things from the veranda. I was halfway down the trail, lantern and bundle in hand, when it occurred to me. Like a match struck, flame to tinder.

The treasure . . .

I stood motionless, thoughts tumbling over one another in a heartbeat.

It's mine now. No one else knows it is here.

But it is stained with blood.

Yet to leave it here is a waste, a shameful waste.

But if you take it, you must share it with your shipmates.

Why? They will squander the treasure and use it for wicked purposes.

But you have taken an oath.

An oath to share equally in any prize captured by the men of the Tempest Galley. *But they did not capture the prize. I did. . . .*

I crept back to the pit, for some reason moving stealthily, as if someone could hear me, as if someone was watching. Setting down my lantern and bundle, I drew my dagger and peered in. I let out my breath, not realizing I'd been holding it. All was as before. Three bodies, stacked one atop the other, arms and legs tangled. The treasure chest lay half hidden under Fist's thigh. It would be simple enough to remove the treasure and bury it elsewhere. I did not relish the thought of rotting bodies being its guardians.

I climbed into the pit, standing on a knee, a shin, my skin crawling. I pushed Fist's thigh aside and tugged on the treasure chest. It was heavier than I'd believed. I tugged again. It moved an inch. Sweat broke out, and I stifled the urge to grab my things and dash pell-mell back to the *Tempest Galley*.

Instead, I reached out of the pit and emptied my canvas hammock, spreading it flat. I next slipped the key from around Fist's hairy neck, every nerve set afire when his head fell back and his tongue lolled out with a gurgly bubble of blood. *Gas*, I told myself, heart skittering like a rabbit's. *Just the expiration of death. Nothing more.*

Hurrying, hands shaking, I unlocked the chest and began scooping great mounds onto my hammock. I emptied the chest and climbed out of the pit.

It took me an hour to bury the treasure, to drag it plus a shovel, plus a lantern, through the jungle. To dig and dig, to stop and tie up my bleeding ear, to dig and dig. I buried the treasure deep, secure once again inside the chest.

Before I left, I paused to memorize my surroundings—each tree, each root, each branch, the way the vines tangled. Tomorrow I would return and draw a map so that I wouldn't forget. By this time, the sky to the east was beginning to lighten. On the way back to the clearing, I memorized my route, carving a notch in a tree trunk every now and then to mark my way.

There was one last thing I needed to do before I could return to the ship.

I had to cover the bodies.

If anyone discovered them, I would have a hard time explaining myself. I'd have a hard enough time as it was, what with my ear sliced, blood covering me, and my feet torn to shreds. Surely there would be a hunt for the missing pirates, wouldn't there?

I stepped back into the clearing for what I hoped would be the last time.

And when I looked into the pit, my blood froze. Where before there had been three bodies, now there were only two.

Fist was gone.

I whirled, dagger in hand. Trees and shadows loomed around the edges of the clearing. Each palm leaf a cutlass. Each vine an arm. Each droplet of water an eye. Already I could feel the blade of a cutlass in my back, piercing and deep.

Fist is alive!

Then I saw it. A trail of blood leading out of the pit and down the path toward the beach. Footsteps in the sand—the dragging footsteps of someone staggering. I dropped to my knees, shaking again like a lily in the wind, forcing myself to reason. Fist was as near death as he could be without being dead. And for all he knew, I was long gone. His only chance to survive would be to return to his shipmates. For now, I believed, I was safe.

I mopped my brow and commenced work.

By the time I finished filling the grave and erasing all traces of my presence from the clearing, I was near famished and drenched with sweat. Sunlight filtered lazily through the trees. Birds twittered and squawked, flitting from tree to tree as if nothing had happened the night before. The underbrush rustled with creatures, but I had stopped jumping out of my skin at every noise, convincing myself that Fist was either stone cold dead on the trail or back aboard the *Defiance*.

I knew he would say nothing of what had happened. After all, he had stolen goods from his shipmates, and the penalty for that was to have his ears and nose slit and to be marooned on a sandbar with only a bullet to put him out of his misery. Nay, he would say nothing. But as I gathered my belongings and headed down the trail, sunlight gradually growing stronger, I knew Fist would be after me. If he did not die of his wound, he would pursue me and torture me until I told him the whereabouts of his treasure.

He could yank my toenails from their roots, roast the bottoms of my feet, and still I would never tell. For once he had the treasure, my life wouldn't be worth spit. He'd slit my throat quick as gunpowder. And besides, the treasure was mine now.

Mine.

CHAPTER 13

As I crawled up the side of the ship and onto the deck, Josiah stood blocking my way.

Already the sun was fierce, the air dripping with moisture. Josiah seemed unaffected by the heat and humidity, for he was fully dressed with a white shirt tucked into his breeches, a kerchief tied round his head, topped with a cocked hat trimmed with galloon. A crossbelt ran from his shoulder across his chest to his hip. Clipped to his crossbelt were three pistols.

"What happened?" he demanded, his gaze taking in my sliced ear. My shirt, both bloody and torn. My legs and feet, scratched, bitten, and swollen.

"Nothing."

"Where were you?"

"What do you care?"

Josiah took me by the arm and steered me around lollygagging pirates. Some of the more industrious of the lot were mending sails or repairing rigging. Others were sleeping in whatever shade they could find, mouths open, snoring. Abe was cutting the head off a chicken. Timothy was playing dice with one of his scoundrel friends. In his cabin, Josiah gave me a drink of liquid fire—toke, he called it—brewed by the locals. Several choking, spluttering gulps later, my head was spinning and I didn't care about anything.

"What happened?" he demanded again.

"Nothing." My voice seemed to come from somewhere else, from far away. My thoughts as well, for I suddenly realized that I could trust Josiah, that I could tell him everything that had happened to me and that he'd still protect me from Fist just as he'd protected me from the pirates when I'd twice tried to betray them. Part of me longed to tell him everything, but instead I clenched my jaw, ordering my thoughts to go away.

"Fist was shot last night. Do you know anything about that?"

The toke nearly loosened my tongue, but then I remembered the treasure. It was mine. "No."

"I suppose you sliced off half your ear with your own cutlass?"

"Uh-huh." The room spun. Josiah looked strange, sounded strange.

He began to wash my wound with a wet rag. I winced and pulled away before letting him continue. Next he patched up my ear with a needle and thread. I just kept drinking toke and denying everything until he finally let me go.

Of course, rumors wormed their way through the crew of the *Tempest Galley* like maggots.

Gideon Fist lay aboard the *Defiance*, near death. Fist had

fought a duel, but no one knew with whom. Some said Josiah; others said the captain of the *Sweet Jamaica*. Others said it had to be Rat Eye and Pete Goe (whom I deduced to be Hairy), for they were now missing and had last been seen with Fist. Fist had likely fought a duel and killed them, everyone said, although he denied it, swearing upon his mother's grave.

I heard someone suggest that maybe it was little Daniel who had fought Fist and won; after all, Daniel *had* come back a bloody mess at the same time Fist was injured. But that suggestion received such a round of hilarity and eye wiping from the crew, Timothy included, that later it became no more than a joke told to cheer someone who was feeling out of sorts.

As for me, I did not care what they thought. In fact, it was best they did not know the truth, for I had the treasure and they did not. Later that afternoon, after Josiah had stitched my ear and after I had rested, I returned to the jungle and scratched the location of the treasure onto the underside of my crossbelt.

Someday, I vowed, *I will return and take my treasure back to Boston, and no one will be the wiser. And, as I promised my father, I will care for Faith and her child . . . if they are still alive.*

Three days after my fight with Fist, the monsoon winds shifted, and the *Tempest Galley,* the *Defiance,* and the *Sweet Jamaica* raised anchor. Together, under a stiff and squally southwest wind, with topsails set, the pirate fleet navigated out of the bottleneck harbor and set sail for the Red Sea.

Aboard the *Tempest Galley* we had 142 men, eleven head of cattle, eighty-nine chickens, fresh fruit and water, barrels of toke, barrels of salt horse, biscuit, and enough weaponry, gunpowder, and ammunition to blow an entire island to the moon. Apparently the pirate at Saint Mary's, the one with the log fort and cannon, dealt in all manner of merchandise, both legal and illegal, and had sold us whatever we needed to accomplish our dirty deeds.

One day, I slid down the mizzen backstay to find Josiah staring at me oddly. His back-staff was in his hands, and he'd been taking a sighting.

"What?" I asked. "Why are you staring at me?"

He shook his head as if to clear it, merely saying, "You remind me of someone I once knew." And back he went to his sighting, adjusting the half cross as he stood against the poop deck rail with his back to the sun.

"Who?"

I held my locket, only realizing that I clutched it when Josiah, without moving his eyes from his task, said, "What's in your locket?"

"My mother's likeness." And for some reason I cannot explain, I opened it and showed it to him. He looked from the miniature to my face and back to the miniature, then returned to his sighting.

"She was very beautiful."

"Aye. She died when I was young." When he said nothing more, I snapped my locket shut. Then, hesitating only a moment, I withdrew the pistol he'd lent me and held it out to him. "Josiah—teach me to shoot."

He set down the back-staff and took the pistol from me, turning it over in his hands, frowning. "You've fired it."

"Aye."

"When?"

I shrugged. "On the island. I tripped and it went off accidentally."

He smiled as if he didn't believe me, as if he somehow knew that I was the one who had shot Fist. "Then 'tis a wonder you still have all your bodily parts, Daniel, my boy," he said, handing me back my pistol. "Caution is as valuable as bravery."

"So, will you?"

He peered through the eyepiece of the back-staff once again, feet spread apart to steady himself. "Every man must know how to care for a pistol, reload it quickly, and use it in battle. If he wishes to live, that is."

I thought of Fist attacking me with his cutlass, the glint of murder in his eyes. The next time we met, I planned to be armed to the teeth, with daggers up my sleeves, cutlass, pistols, and enough powder and lead to send him to the devil. "So, will you?"

"Of course."

Hot days, they were. The *Sweet Jamaica* and the *Defiance* sailed in our wake, their yards of canvas filled with the steady breeze, billowing white against the sapphire blue of the Indian Ocean. Three ships filled with over four hundred men, out to make their fortunes.

At first, Caesar taught me swordsmanship as usual, while Josiah instructed me on how to use the pistol. But then one day in the middle of a drill on loading my pistol, Josiah drew his cutlass and pointed it at my throat. I felt my eyes widen, staring at him across the expanse of steel. "Always be ready, Daniel, my boy. You never know who might be waiting for an opportunity to kill you."

From that day forward, Josiah taught me all manner of fighting. Daggers, hand to hand. Cutlasses, on a flat deck, on a heaving deck, dangling from the shrouds, two against one, three against one. Pistol with cutlass, one in each hand. *Clash, bang*—everybody watching. By the end of each session, I had long since discarded my shirt. My skin, darkened by the sun, glistened with sweat. As always, Josiah seemed unaffected, his skin still pale as winter, his white linen shirt and knee breeches not even damp. He'd shove his pistol into his sash, saying, "Enough for today."

One fine day, as clouds scudded across the sky like a fleet of ships, I circled Josiah with a dagger in each hand, waiting for an opening to attack. Despite the breeze, the air was as stifling as a jungle's. We'd been practicing for over an hour, and he'd already beaten me a dozen times over. Now we circled again like animals, watching, waiting, my every nerve tense and ready to spring. When Josiah glanced away, a second only, I sprang, right dagger thrusting down, left dagger sweeping up. He caught me across the neck. I didn't even see it coming. One second I was charging, the next I was on the ground, gagging, dagger at my throat.

"Surrender, Daniel."

I took a moment to recover my wits. Then I smiled and said hoarsely, "I never surrender when my finger's on the trigger."

Josiah looked to where my pistol, still in its sash, was pointed at his belly, my finger, indeed, on the trigger. Suddenly he barked with laughter, released his hold, and offered me a hand, helping me to my feet. "Well done, Daniel, my boy!"

Still laughing, looking pleased, he clapped me around the shoulders while I grinned with satisfaction, having bested him at last. Suddenly my grin froze rigidly and I realized what I was doing, how friendly I was becoming with the murderer of my father. Guilt slammed through me like a cannon blast and I roughly shrugged out of his grasp. His laughter ceased abruptly. I picked up my daggers from the deck and hardened my voice. "Just because I'm learning to fight doesn't mean I'm a pirate. I still despise you for what you did and will see you hang."

Then, to my shock, Josiah's expression grew dark and he thrust his face into mine. Against my will, I took a step backward. "No one hangs Josiah Black," he whispered between clenched teeth. "No one. Not even you, Daniel Markham. And I will kill anyone who tries." So saying, he sheathed his daggers and strode aft.

I suddenly became aware of everyone staring at me, the rigging slapping in the wind, the gurgle of water, the bellow of a cow 'tween decks. Sheathing my daggers as well, I sauntered to the fore companionway as if nothing were the matter and went below.

I threaded my way past cannon, past the galley oars set inboard except in light winds, around barrels, coils of rope, jumbles of canvas, chicken coops, pens filled with cattle. Rats scuttled in the darkened corners. Chickens cackled. Water sloshed against the hull. The heat made the stink almost unbearable, as if the air I breathed dripped with manure, piss, bilgewater, and mildew.

After stowing my pistol and cutlass in my sea chest, I climbed into my hammock, strung between the cattle pen and a twelve-pounder cannon, and held my locket in my hand, staring upward at the beams overhead.

I tried to visualize my father's face beneath his periwig, the spectacles perched on the end of his nose. I tried to remember how he looked whenever he took a pinch of snuff. I tried to hear his voice, pleading with me to look after Faith, telling me I was a good son. But all I saw was Josiah Black, looking pleased, laughing, his arm clapped around my shoulders.

I wanted to howl, to wail, to ridiculously beat my chest, but instead I squeezed my eyes closed, pressing back the sting of tears.

Forgive me, Father.

I felt a movement—a brush of whiskers and a wisp of foul breath. In a wild heartbeat my dagger was in my hand, the blade glinting in the semidarkness. "Who goes there?" I hissed.

"Truce! Truce! 'Tis I, Basil Higgins, the quartermaster! I come unarmed. I've only a wish to speak with ye."

I lowered my blade and peered at him. Of all the pirates aboard, Basil was one I believed I could trust. It was his duty as quartermaster to act as mediator between captain and crew, to be sure power and greed didn't go to anyone's head, most especially the captain's. It was his task to oversee and divide the booty, to manage provisions and supplies, to see that all was fair. Like the captain, he was elected by the men. "What is it?"

"Well, Daniel, I don't quite know how to say this—but what I mean is . . . well, I think that you're a good boy." He ran a hand over his whiskers, his voice as deep and raspy as always. "I remembers when ye was a little lad sitting on my lap, and I thought to myself, now there's a good boy. A real good boy. Anyway, what I come to talk to ye about is, well . . ." Basil coughed and cleared his throat. "Well, a rather delicate matter."

"Delicate?" I didn't know pirates knew such words.

"You see, Daniel, Captain Black, he's a sensitive man."

I choked back a laugh.

"Don't get me wrong, he's ruthless too. Aye, very ruthless. I've seen him toss a fellow overboard because he was wasting air and had bad breath besides. I've seen him torture a merchant captain till he cried like a baby and told him where his wife and all the treasure was hid. So what I'm trying to say is, for you to be embarrassing him in front of his crew likely don't sit too good with his constitution, him being sensitive and ruthless. Are you getting my drift, lad?"

I thrust out my jaw, tears stinging my eyes once again. "I'll avenge my father if I choose. Any man aboard this ship would do the same. If he's even half a man, that is."

"Now, that may well be, but I'm warning you. Don't be too hasty with your judgments."

90

"What do you mean?"

"All I can say is, there's things in Josiah's past that you don't know nothing about."

"His past?" I asked, strangely curious.

But Basil pulled away, leaving my hammock swinging, his one massive eyebrow scrunching in the middle. "I've already said too much. I've crossed me bounds, I have, but 'tis my job as the keeper of the peace to sometimes cross the boundaries, and I hope you'll forgive me. You and Josiah both." And then he was gone.

CHAPTER
14

$\mathcal{T}$he weather continued pleasant, and we made good speed toward the Red Sea.

Each night, scores of flying fish landed aboard and flapped about in the scuppers until Abe collected them in his bucket. Ofttimes I helped him clean the fish and fry them in oil, my appetite growing with the smell of fresh fish drifting through the ship as the sun rose and the men began to stir.

Despite my desire to believe otherwise, I had learned long ago that what had appeared to be a ship of chaos, filled with men too lazy to lift more than a bottle of rum, was in actual fact a well-run alliance. Unlike a merchant crew with maybe fifteen to twenty-five men who worked four hours on and four hours off day in and day out, a pirate crew of 150 men shared the burden of work so that at any one time the vast majority of men were indeed lounging about and shooting the breeze.

Like the others, I was required to work no more than four hours per day but often chose to work more. Whenever I worked, I pretended that this was a merchant ship or a navy ship, that I was an able-bodied seaman, and that life was somehow normal again. Or I pretended that I was Daniel Markham, gentleman adventurer and seeker of revenge, which I was, of course, battling every villain who ever lived.

One day I sat upon the bulwarks, cutlass in hand, wind in my face, and realized to my surprise that I had come to love the sea and even the *Tempest Galley,* despite the despicable morality of the ship's company. So, in between my daily fight lessons with Josiah, and upon my request, Basil now taught me seamanship. How to tie a bowline, a rolling hitch, a sheet bend. The manner of ships' bells. How to handle the helm and box the compass. How to trim the sails for any tack. What to do when I heard the cry, "All hands wear ship!" and "Stand by to set cro'jack! Let go the brails, haul out!"

Of course I wondered about what Basil had said to me. *There's things in Josiah's past that you don't know nothing about,* he'd said. *What things?* I wondered. *What did Basil mean? And what does it have to do with me?* I asked Basil about Josiah while we were aloft, reefing the fore course because the *Sweet Jamaica* was falling too far behind. "Why did he become a pirate?"

"Captain Black, he was a privateer commissioned to hunt down ships of England's enemies. Only thing was, when Captain Black returned after a year or so with his treasure, the government denied ever having given him a commission and locked him up instead. It was an injustice, Daniel. A terrible injustice."

"Why did they deny having given him a commission?"

Basil shrugged. "Can't say."

"What happened?"

"He escaped, of course, and took up the life again. Only this time he didn't have a commission and targeted the governor's ships. The king's ships as well. They don't take too kindly to that, you know."

"But what did you mean when you said there's things in Josiah's past that I don't know anything about?"

"I'll say no more about it," Basil replied, seeming to seal his lips shut even as he said so. "There are things of which it is better not to speak."

And indeed, no matter how many times I begged or cajoled, now Basil acted as if he didn't know what I was talking about.

One night, as the half moon carved the black sky like a scimitar, I asked Timothy what he knew of Josiah. Had he heard anything? Some secret in his past, maybe? We both stood at the bow, the bowsprit pointing into the darkness. Beneath us, wave caps shimmered moon-silver as the *Tempest Galley* sped along, close-hauled on a freshening breeze that blew us day and night toward the Red Sea.

Timothy didn't answer me right away, instead taking a swallow from his cup. "Drink?" he offered, holding out his cup to me. His hand trembled, and even in the moonlight I could see bags under his eyes.

I shook my head. "You're not looking so well."

He brushed his hand through his mop of hair. "Can't help it. Toke's getting low. Rum's all out. I'm getting dry, Daniel, awful dry, and my head's busting. Can't hardly think straight anymore."

"Maybe you should stop drinking so much. Look what it's doing to you."

"Maybe you should mind your own bloody business," he replied, his voice high and sharp. "You sound like a bloody minister. Or bloody God on his bloody throne."

For the last couple of weeks, Timothy had grown more and

more irritable. I sighed, supposing it was like he said—the rum was all out and the toke was getting low. "Just trying to help."

"Well, you can stop now. You aren't my mother."

"Don't you miss her?"

Timothy looked away. "Of course."

"Don't you think she worries about you?"

"Believe me, once I come home a wealthy man, she'll forget all her worries. I'll buy her the biggest house in Boston, dresses fit for a queen, and anything else she wants. I'll take care of her, you can be sure of that. She'll never again have to worry about being sent to the poorhouse."

"Do you really think you'll come home a wealthy man?"

Timothy looked at me, eyes narrowed. "What do you mean?"

I shrugged and looked away, pretending this was just nonchalant conversation. "Just wondering how good Captain Black really is, that's all. Just wondering if he's good enough to make everybody on this ship a wealthy man." It wasn't what I really wanted to know, but it was good enough for starters.

"Bloody fire, Daniel, where have you been? Sulking around with your head up your backside, likely. Everyone knows Captain Black's the finest pirate captain that ever lived. There's a reward on him for five hundred British pounds sterling, dead or alive."

I did not have to pretend surprise. "Five hundred pounds?" *Now that would be a fortune indeed!*

"They say that once Captain Black fired a broadside on a fleet of merchant ships at anchor, and that each of their captains was struck with a cannonball. Then he went aboard each ship, and they were so scared out of their wits that he just helped himself to whatever he wanted. It was a fortune intended for the king of England. Of course, Captain Black could have retired, but he didn't. Not him. And every man aboard his ship was so rich they never had to work again."

"Sounds like poppycock to me."

Timothy's skinny shoulders rose and fell in a shrug. "Well, you can think what you want, but as for myself, I intend to have a piece of that sort of poppycock."

As Timothy wandered away, I chewed my lip, wondering. *Is Josiah really such a wanted man? Did he steal a fortune intended for the king? Am I really in the hands of the most infamous pirate in the world?*

I asked other people about Josiah too. I asked Caesar as we were drilling on the twelve-pounder cannon; I asked Will Putt as we set the stuns'ls because the *Sweet Jamaica* was now too far ahead. I asked just about everyone I had a chance to ask. I even joined Timothy and his dice-playing scoundrels just to hear the talk. Some said Josiah was a determined man, fearless, the best in battle, the finest swordsman, someone they would willingly follow anywhere. Others told yarns so fantastical, as if Josiah had wings and could fly, that they were more or less a load of bilge in my opinion.

But no one, it seemed—save Basil Higgins, whose lips were duly sealed—knew the things about Josiah's past of which it was better not to speak.

On the twenty-third day of July, 1697, the fleet hove to in a harbor at Perim Island, located in the narrow Bab el-Mandeb at the southern end of the Red Sea. The strait was only twenty miles across, the island a perfect base for monitoring traffic both entering and exiting the Red Sea.

Uninhabited, bare, sandy, strewn with hilly rocks that reared like yellow scars into the azure sky, Perim Island was a dismal affair. The air was baking hot and dry as dust. The occasional wind gust blew sand into our eyes, drying the backs of our throats and stinging our skin. With the raising of the green silk flag on the main halyard of the *Tempest Galley*, all men from the three ships repaired to shore for a general council. I sat on the sand next to Timothy, shirt off, ducking my head whenever I caught sight of Gideon Fist.

Aye, Fist had lived. I'd first seen him a few weeks earlier, pacing the deck of the *Defiance*, steps slow and shuffling at first, day by day seeming to gather both strength and speed. My disappointment was acute. I'd beseeched, prayed, cajoled, begged the heavens to let Fist die, to send him to the hell he deserved, but alas, heaven remained unconvinced on that account.

"Men, like many of you, I've been on the Round before," said Josiah, his voice flat and dull in the smothering heat. "It's a well-known fact that each year the pilgrim fleet coordinates their departure from Mecca with the monsoon seasons. And once they set sail for India, they will have no choice but to sail past us. That, my men, is the moment for which we have been waiting, for which we have sailed thousands of miles to attend. And we must be ready."

While Josiah was talking, Fist had moved to stand beside him—two pirate captains, side by side. If Josiah knew Fist was there, he made no show of it.

"Weapons must be kept sharp and clean," Josiah was saying. "Ammunition dry. Every man ready for action at a moment's notice. We must employ ourselves making grenadoes and stink pots and preparing the cannon. Decks must be kept clear for ease in fighting, grappling hooks at the ready. . . ."

Slowly, Fist swiveled his head and turned his treacherous gaze directly on me. He neither blinked nor twitched, and it was almost as if I could hear his thoughts—rank thoughts reeking like the bilge. *I'll get you, puppy. I'll rip out your tongue and eat your eyes. I'll boil your innards and hang your hide to dry. I'll make you wish you'd never been born.*

A fresh sweat broke out on my forehead that had nothing to

do with the heat. I looked away, absently patting my crossbelt, the treasure map scratched on its underside. I didn't hear much else of what Josiah said, scarce noted the cheers and roars of the pirates at the conclusion, the blasts of pistol fire.

At my first opportunity, I shipped back to the *Tempest Galley* aboard the pinnace. Even as I put my back to the oars, even as I saw Josiah wring Fist's hand, saying that it was good to see him up and around at last, Fist's gaze was upon me, boring black holes through my heart.

I wore four pistols at all times—cleaned, primed, loaded, and ready to fire, two hooked to my crossbelt, two shoved in my sash, along with my cartouche box, filled with twenty-three charges and bullets. Hanging from my crossbelt at my left hip, my cutlass, shining, honed so sharp it could slice a feather floating in midair. A boarding ax, short like a hatchet, shoved in my sash. In my waistbelt, two sheathed daggers, double-edged—one at the small of my back, one at my right hip.

I practiced drawing my dagger. Again. Again. Faster. Stealthier. Flinging it at the mainmast from ten paces over and over, until it stuck fast, quivering, every time. Until Basil finally ran me off, saying I'd ruin the mast before I was finished.

The three ships patrolled the strait, returning to Perim at nightfall. Fist captained the *Defiance* once again, and whenever our two ships passed I ducked out of sight behind the bulwarks.

And after that first day, I never went ashore again. I stayed aboard the *Tempest Galley,* well remembering the danger I was in and what might happen if Gideon Fist caught me alone. As it was, Fist came aboard the *Tempest Galley* multiple times, supposedly to speak with Josiah, who was the fleet commander. But each time, his gaze roved about, seeking me. Always I surrounded myself with a half dozen or more men, suddenly finding interest in dice.

As July passed into August, whispers circulated like gusts of hot air. The southwest monsoon was beginning to wane, and the pilgrim fleet would pass any day now, any hour, thirty ships or more. With no more defenses than a child, each ship would be loaded to the gunwales with jewels, silver and gold coins, coffee, and wine, its cabins filled with wealthy passengers, each dressed like royalty.

Meanwhile, Timothy and I assembled grenadoes. We packed gunpowder and small shot into hollow balls of lead, with a fuse ready to be lit and thrown. (I planned to *accidentally* throw the grenadoes into the water during battle, where they would fizzle and die. Unless, of course, I saw Fist coming to get me, in which case I prayed for the accuracy to toss a grenado down his throat.)

Then, for three days, we choked and gagged on the fumes that wisped aboard. Abe Corner stood on the shore, bandanna tied around his nose and mouth, stirring a giant cauldron filled with pitch, tar, saltpeter, sulfur, and other such stinky substances. So diligent was Abe in his task of making stink pots, flinging himself away occasionally for a good juicy cry and a blowing of his nose, that the crew got together, myself included, and voted him an extra share of the booty. He smiled and waved at us from shore, stumping around on his wooden leg, snuffling loudly, eyes red as the devil.

One day, following a sword fight lesson that left me helpless as a struggling fly, lying flat on my back panting and groaning, Josiah withdrew the point of his cutlass from my chest and said, "You've improved, Daniel."

The sun blazed behind his head, hurting my eyes. "I—I have?"

"Aye. You ducked when you should have, advanced when you saw the opportunity, and beat me back with a strength and skill you've not possessed before."

"But you won. Again."

I saw the glint of a smile. "Your day is coming. You already surpass most men on this ship—most men in the fleet, for that matter, who count on their brute strength rather than their skill and agility."

He helped me to my feet, and I sheathed my cutlass, my arm trembling with fatigue. Despite myself, I felt pleased under his approval. *Can I really beat most men in the fleet? Including Fist?*

For the rest of that day, I admit, I strutted about the deck. I strutted until nightfall, until I finally collapsed with a clank of weapons on the deck next to Timothy, who rolled over sleepily, muttering something about Daniel acting like an idiot.

I drifted into a deep sleep, dreaming of fancy footwork, flashing swords, daggers quivering in the mainmast, when someone shook me awake. I sat up, groggily rubbing my eyes. Timothy had been shaking me a long time, it seemed, for everyone else was up though it was still the dead of night.

"Wake up, Daniel, wake up. It's the fleet. The pilgrim fleet. It slipped past us in the dark."

$\mathcal{W}$hispered orders whipped about like fire in a whirlwind—from Josiah on the quarterdeck, from Basil in the waist, echoed from one man to the next.

"Make sail!"

"Aloft sail loosers!"

"Lead along topsail sheets and halyards, jib halyards!"

The deck reverberated with the trample of feet. I heard the clank of iron, coils of rope slapping the deck, the clap of sail as yards of canvas unfurled overhead.

I had no time to wonder how many ships had slipped by, or how big they were, or whether or not they had escaped us entirely, for I flung myself down the companionway to my station at the oar. Timothy was already there, and I slipped in beside him. There were twenty-three sweeps on both port and starboard, making a total of ninety-two men who grunted and strained as they pushed and pulled to the rhythm of Caesar's drum.

Overhead, still, the deck thumped with footsteps, until finally there was no noise except the deep beat of the drum, the breathing of the men, the groan of timbers, the slosh of water, and the creak of oars. The swaying lanterns cast a sickly yellow light through the masses of glistening, stinking bodies.

And with each beat of the drum, words echoed through my head. Hated words. *Cowardice or deserting the ship in battle is punishable by death. . . .*

I had taken an oath upon the Bible against cowardice. Yet I did not truly wish to participate in this act of piracy, for piracy was no more than thievery and sometimes even murder, and I was neither thief nor murderer. And never had I taken an oath to commit either. It was therefore necessary to appear courageous, fearless, as if I was born to the life of villainy from the moment I first drew breath, while at the same time doing no harm.

Playing this game, this charade, was like dancing atop a dagger while trying not to fall. And the thinking of it caused a churning in my stomach.

O God, O merciful God.

After the *Tempest Galley* had gained sufficient speed, we hauled our sweeps inboard and rejoined the rest of the crew on the upper deck.

I spent the next hour in fervent prayer. Checking my weapons, the cannon, praying, praying, my prayers like a sour taste in my mouth.

Just then, Basil whispered harshly from the bowsprit, "Not a noise, now. 'Tis time for the cat to catch a mouse."

I spied the straggler, visible under a half moon, sailing ahead of us by no more than a cable's length, seeming all alone. Even with most of her sail set, she appeared sluggish, like a plump old woman waddling along. The *Tempest Galley* would be on her in mere minutes. She appeared unaware of the danger lurking off her starboard quarter, unaware of the scores of cutthroats crouched behind the bulwarks or standing in the shrouds, ready to shoot anyone who might be tempted to sound the alarm.

Behind us, there was no sign of either the *Defiance* or the *Sweet Jamaica*. We had outsailed them both.

I hunched behind the bulwarks myself, scrunched between Timothy and Caesar, Caesar's teeth gleaming eerily in the moonlight. Beside me, Timothy whispered, "Not long now, Daniel, and we'll be rich men. It'll be worth it in the end, believe me." His eyes were wild, rounded, tinged with both excitement and fear. "Pray they're loaded to the gunwales with gold. And while you're at it," he added, "say a prayer for me as well."

"Aye. Have a care for yourself, Timothy."

"You too."

I wiped my hands on my breeches and fingered the hilt of my cutlass, wishing it were already over, dreading what was to come.

Then I heard the scrape of a boot beside me. It was Josiah, crouched down, his hand gripping my arm almost painfully. "If anything goes wrong, Daniel," he whispered in my ear, "stay near me. And watch your back." Without waiting for a reply, he moved away.

"Stand ready, men," Josiah said softly.

I saw the hulk of a ship looming above me, so close I could have reached out and grazed her sides. I heard the creak of her timbers, heard Josiah whisper, "Boarders away!"

Out from the *Tempest Galley* soared a dozen or more hooks, snagging the rigging. The instant the lines were hauled tight, pirates swarmed aboard the other ship, silent as moonlight.

I placed the blade of my dagger in my teeth and followed—swinging on a rope across the watery chasm, onto the deck, dagger instantly in hand. The pirates had already captured the helmsman and three other men on deck. They were stuffing their mouths with gags, tying their hands behind their backs, weapons in a pile at their feet.

Josiah signaled to several of his men, glanced at me, and then strode to the door of the captain's cabin beneath the quarterdeck, cast open the door, and entered. I hurried after, blinking back sweat, wanting to prevent any bloodshed. Truthfully, I did not know what Josiah would do.

I entered the cabin on the heels of Basil Higgins, Caesar, and Will Putt, hearing Timothy breathing behind me. The cabin was dimly lit, a single candle burning in a glass-encased lantern that rocked gently back and forth. Beneath the lantern was the captain's table. Playing cards lay strewn across the table and scattered across the floor. The captain of the ship sat on a velvet settee behind the table, cards slipping from his hand as Josiah leaned across the table, pistol cocked and leveled at the captain's face. "Surrender your ship."

There were two others who had been playing cards with the captain. Pistols were aimed at each of their heads as well. A pipe dangling from one of their mouths fell and clattered to the floor.

Upon Josiah's words, the captain blinked, licked his lips, and said in a heavy accent, "Yes, yes. Yes, yes."

Josiah smiled, stood back, removed his cocked hat, and gave a sweeping bow—whether mocking or not, I did not know. "You are a wise captain," he said. "Rest assured we shall treat you and your passengers with honor and safety." To the rest of us he said, "Open up the holds, boys. Let's see what she has in store for us."

And so we took possession of the *Jedda* without bloodshed, without a shot being fired, and with much pleasantry, if truth be known. My relief was so intense that I felt like singing to the heavens.

The crew and passengers were herded to the bow and kept under guard, while the pirates swarmed over the ship, prodding every cuddy, crevice, and corner for treasure.

I volunteered to stand guard over the crew and passengers, as it was my intention to both protect them from wanton violence and to reassure them. "If you stay still, no one will be hurt," I kept saying, smiling, hoping they could understand me despite the obvious language barrier. Men, women, some children, most of them dark-skinned—Indian, I presumed—were dressed in bright silks and sleeping clothes, some weeping in each other's arms.

There is nothing to fear so long as you do nothing rash, I thought.

Several passengers looked European, including one of the men who'd been playing cards with the captain. I pointed at myself and said, "Daniel Markham," and then pointed at them and asked them their names. I asked them if they spoke English, but they just stared at me blankly, saying nothing.

I wanted to tell them that if they were quiet, the pirates would take what they wanted and leave them safely behind. That it would not do to make the pirates angry. That I would protect them with my very life if need be. But such words would be wasted upon ears that could not understand, and so I gave up trying and just stood with my arms crossed, a pistol in each hand to protect them against rogues and robbers, trying to look tough enough so that none could accuse me of shirking in my piratical duties, of not fulfilling my oath.

I was dancing on the point of a dagger quite well, in my opinion.

Meanwhile, the hatches were thrown open and lanterns brightly lit. Men shifted the cargo from the *Jedda* to the *Tempest Galley*. Chests, barrels, crates—all were filled with finery and riches. There was much laughter, backslapping, grinning, even giggling. One stupid oaf gleefully shot off his pistol, immediately receiving a cuff on the head from Josiah. "Fool!" he cried. "There are more ships to capture this night. And if we do not alarm them to our presence, we can take them as easily as we took this one. Now hurry—there is still much to do, and we must be on our way."

In the midst of transferring the cargo, the *Defiance* luffed under the *Jedda*'s stern, the *Sweet Jamaica* not far behind. I couldn't hear what transpired between Fist and Josiah, but soon after, the *Defiance* fell off the wind and sailed after the vanished fleet with the *Sweet Jamaica* in her wake, sails and towering masts dimly outlined in the predawn light.

The sun was midway up the sky by the time we took leave of the *Jedda*, speeding after the *Defiance* and the *Sweet Jamaica* with all sails set.

Like many others, when I wasn't on duty, I fetched a few hours' sleep on the fo'c'sle deck, exhausted from our night's adventure. Though we had captured a great quantity of wine, Josiah had ordered that there would be no drinking until we finished hunting down the fleet. We were still on battle alert—on the chase—and so long as we were, Josiah had ultimate command, with the power to drub or kill any man who disobeyed.

Night had fallen, and I was asleep on the fo'c'sle deck, curled into a ball, when Timothy shook me awake again. "Daniel. There's something you've got to see."

I heard a low murmur coming from the waist deck and scrambled down the companionway behind Timothy, yawning, wondering what the fuss was about. A clot of pirates stood near the mainmast. Timothy wormed his way through the crowd, tugging me by the wrist.

When we reached the inner circle, I gasped.

Bracelets, necklaces, crowns, and scepters encrusted with rubies, emeralds, and diamonds sparkled in the lantern light. Gold coins, silver coins, loose jewels . . .

"'Tis a king's ransom," whispered Timothy. "We're all bloody rich."

"Aye," agreed Basil, who sat gazing up at the enormous pile, his eyes glittering like sapphires. "More than any man could earn in a hundred lifetimes of labor. Two hundred lifetimes, maybe. And this is only part of the booty. The rest of it, mates, delicious booty all of it, is below."

As a body, the pirates moved closer, the circle tight. The heat was stifling, our breathing loud.

I knew I should leave; I knew that this was none of my business, none of my concern. But my feet seemed to have grown roots, and I could no more move than I could fly.

Over the next half hour, we watched as Basil divided the treasure. There were many suggestions as to how he should do it: move a ruby from this pile to that one . . . exchange the giant emerald for the hundred little diamonds . . . three necklaces were worth one crown. But Basil ignored everybody, did it his own way, and soon little piles emerged.

Then he began calling names, and each man duly came forward, accepting his portion without complaint. Man after man. Timothy went forward when his name was called, holding open a canvas bag into which Basil poured his share. When Timothy came back to stand beside me, to my surprise, tears glistened upon his cheeks.

Then Basil said, "Daniel Markham."

I turned toward Basil, blinking hard, saying nothing, realizing everyone was watching me.

"Come get your share, lad."

I opened my mouth to refuse, but nothing came out.

I am not a pirate. . . .

If you do not take it, they will simply divide your share among themselves. It would be as good as wasted upon rum, gambling, women, and other such wicked debaucheries. . . .

But I am not a thief. . . .

Think of Faith, think of her child. You must care for them someday. It is right that you do this. Much good can come of it instead of much evil.

Besides, no blood was shed. . . .

No blood . . .

I realized I had stepped forward. Someone thrust a canvas bag into my hands. I held it open, treasure tinkling as the bag grew heavy, heavy . . .

For you, Faith.

For the next day and night we sailed hard across the Gulf of Aden toward India, every stitch of canvas full and bellied. On the morning of the second day, just as a pale stream of sunlight pierced the horizon, the lookout cried, "Sail ho! One point off the leeward bow!" After looking through his eyeglass atop the fore crosstrees, Josiah reported that the *Defiance* and the *Sweet Jamaica* were chasing two ships of the pilgrim fleet. They were miles ahead, and we would be on them by midafternoon.

Then, surprising us all, bold as brass, Timothy drew his cutlass and ran to the rail, hair flogging in the wind. He screamed like an animal, high-pitched and shrill. His eyes bulged. He swiped his cutlass through the air. "We'll get you, you bloody devils! Run away from us, will you!"

There followed a moment of stunned silence before men drew their weapons and screamed alongside Timothy—a bloodthirsty chorus. Pistols banged. The air swirled with smoke.

And upon Timothy's words, the roar of the pirates, the pistol fire, an excitement unlike any I'd ever known raced up my spine, cool and prickling.

O God, O God, forgive me.

CHAPTER
16

$\mathcal{S}$ometime after high noon, after we downed a hurried meal of salt pork and biscuit, we passed both the *Sweet Jamaica* and the *Defiance*. Four or five cable lengths ahead of us sailed the two pilgrim ships, the closest being the *Surat Merchant*.

She was broad across her beam, armed with thirty guns. Swirls of gold surrounded the high stern windows. Atop her mainmast flew a flag—green, with two crossed golden scimitars. Basil said it was the flag of the Surat grand mogul.

Even at the distance, I glimpsed people glancing back at us over the transom. I well imagined their terror. I well imagined the commands, the preparations, the weeping among the passengers, the secreting away of jewels and money in the hopes that the pirates wouldn't be any the wiser.

All the excitement I'd felt when Timothy had issued his bloodthirsty scream had vanished in the heat of the day. Instead, I felt nothing but shame for my momentary weakness and a pity for these people who were about to be attacked. I prayed they would be wise and surrender quickly, for then they could expect quarter, mercy, even gallant treatment if the mood so struck the pirates. But if they did not surrender . . .

I mopped the sweat from my face with my kerchief and then tied it around my head. For the hundredth time I checked my weapons—my pistols, my boarding ax, my cartouche box, my daggers, my cutlass. Both of us shirtless, Timothy and I stood on the upper deck in plain view. There was no sense hiding behind the bulwarks, for the two ships were no doubt well aware of who chased them.

The powder box was positioned nearby. Timothy and I had filled it earlier with twenty-five shots. Should we need to fire our long guns, we were to be powder monkeys, hauling the shots from the powder box to our respective cannon crews. The swivel gun in the bow was already loaded, primed, and ready to fire. Basil stood beside it, awaiting orders.

The *Surat Merchant* rose and plunged through the swells, whitewater dashing her rails. But her mad dash to escape was futile, for there was no ship so fast as the *Tempest Galley*.

Three cable lengths. Two. One.

Josiah cried, "To your battle stations, men!"

Weapons were checked for the thousandth time—pistols crammed into sashes, hooked onto crossbelts, tied to the ends of long ribbons and draped about the neck.

All was ready.

All waited.

"Ready to fire bow chaser!" Josiah ordered.

Slowly . . . slowly we drew closer, the *Surat Merchant* now but one hundred feet off the leeward bow.

"Fire!"

And with Josiah's command, Basil struck the match to the vent, shouting, "Give fire!" then ducking and covering his ears. Orange fire burst from the bow gun, and a loud boom split the air. We all watched as the iron ball sailed harmlessly over the *Surat Merchant*'s stern.

A warning shot.

Surrender or else, it said.

We held our breaths, waiting for the merchant ship to turn head to wind so we could board her.

I tightened my grip on my cutlass, tasting the salt of my sweat.

With no warning, flame and smoke burst out of her two stern gun ports. I stood stupidly, half wondering what was happening when, a second later I heard the boom of cannon, followed by the sound of shot whistling overhead. A cannonball punched through the main course. Another glanced off the foremast with a sharp crack of timber. I cursed and ducked behind the powder box before I realized that if any shot hit the powder box, I'd be blown to a million pieces. As suddenly as it had begun, there followed a silence.

Josiah drew his cutlass and jumped atop the bulwarks, hanging on to the shrouds. Rage darkened his normally pale features. He pointed his cutlass at the *Surat Merchant*. "Run up the bloody flag and prepare to fire a broadside down their miserable throats! There will be no quarter this day!"

A flag the color of blood was raised on the main halyard. No mercy, it meant. To the hair-raising screams and curses of pirates, I laid aside my weapons and went to work as a powder monkey.

Soon we were directly abeam the merchant ship. The deck shivered as flame and cannonballs belched from the *Tempest Galley*. My bones rattled and my ears rang, like a punch in the gut and a box on the ears at the same time. I staggered back to the powder box for more charge, breathing smoke, teeth gritty with gunpowder.

Timothy was all smiles, dipping his arm into the powder box. "Another treasure, Daniel. Do you hear me? We're going to roll in it tonight. A hundred diamond rings for every one of my mother's fingers and toes."

Again I heard the thunderous roar from the *Surat Merchant*.

Whump! A shot hit the bulwarks in a spray of splinters. Someone screamed. Another shot dropped in the ocean below, showering a cannon crew with water. Droplets hissed and danced on the cannon's hot barrel. "Blood and thunder!" Will Putt yelled, wiping his eyes. "Heathen dogs! See if they get me wet!"

"Fire!" shouted Josiah, and again the deck trembled beneath me as I covered my ears against the barrage. Once the sound began to fade, Josiah cried, "Stand by the braces! We'll ram her with our bowsprit and board her!"

We soon left the *Surat Merchant* behind us on our leeward quarter. Behind the *Surat Merchant*, I saw the *Defiance*, bloody flag flying atop her mainmast, fire a shot off her bows—a puff of smoke in the distance, a faraway boom. Ahead of us, the other merchant ship sailed onward, scarce looking back at her beleaguered companion.

"Helmsman, hard to starboard!" commanded Josiah. "Brace in the yards, men!" The *Tempest Galley* turned, stern to wind, her bowsprit now pointed like a sword at the approaching *Surat Merchant*. "Prepare for impact!"

For a moment, all was silent as we watched the *Surat Merchant* plow through the water.

Then someone dangling from the rigging, dagger in hand, cried, "Death!"

One hundred and forty pirates erupted with piercing screams, battle cries, and the chant: "Death! Death! Death!"

Pirates swarmed the bulwarks, waving their weapons above their heads. Pistols flashed in the afternoon sun. Cutlasses gleamed. Eyes glinted from beneath blood-red kerchiefs. The deep beat of a drum pounded through my heart. Fiddles, flutes, and an accordion wailed and screeched—discordant and ugly. Gooseflesh rushed over my skin. Shivers clawed down my spine.

Death! Death! Death!

I stood at the rail on the fo'c'sle deck, watching in gathering horror as the two ships drew closer . . . closer . . . bent upon a collision course. The *Surat Merchant* tried to change course, but she was too sluggish, there was not enough time. . . .

"Death!" shrieked Timothy from beside me. He lit and tossed a grenado. It fell short, hissing into the water.

I drew my cutlass, my heart in my throat.

Forty feet . . .

Death! Death! Death!

Thirty . . .

Men heaved grenadoes and stink pots aboard the merchant ship. Explosions erupted. I saw a man fly through the air, musket still in hand, into the water below.

Just then, flame and smoke burst from one of the swivel guns on the *Surat Merchant*'s bow.

Whump!

Death cry cut short, Timothy flew backward, hit.

"Timothy!" I cried.

He lay against the foremast.

Death! Death! Death!

Timothy held his innards in his hands. He blinked and stared at his innards, then at me, his face a mask of disbelief.

"My God! No!" I knelt beside him. Tried to stuff his guts back into his belly. They were soft, slimy, and hot. *Oh, God! They won't fit! There's too many of them!* "Don't die, Timothy! Don't die!"

His mouth moved wordlessly. Open. Closed. Open. Then, "My mother. Tell her . . . tell her . . . I . . . ." His eyes rolled back in his head.

"No!" I shrieked.

Suddenly the ships collided. I fell to the deck, stinging my cheek, my dagger gouging my side. Timothy flopped over, his lifeless eyes staring at me, a small bloody cannonball lodged in the foremast behind him. Pirates rushed past us, swarming aboard the *Surat Merchant*. I stood and picked up my fallen cutlass, hands slippery with Timothy's blood.

And I turned with the others and surged over the bowsprit and aboard the merchant ship, cutlass held high, a scream ripping from my throat.

Death! Death! Death!

CHAPTER 17

$\mathcal{A}$ mad rush of bodies.

Into the swirling smoke.

It was as if time stood still—I saw the gaping mouths, howling death. The daggers, cutlasses, pistols clutched in every hand. The intensity in every eye. The brightly colored clothes, some already stained with blood. I smelled the gunpowder, the sweat, the sulfur from the stink pots, the exhilaration, the fear.

Then it was as if time rushed forward, faster, faster. A blur of pirates, running, running, arms waving, swords flashing. Indian soldiers, hundreds of them, turbaned, drawing cutlasses, firing muskets. A collision of pirates and soldiers. The blast of smoke. Of flame. Screams. The man beside me falling backward, punched through the chest with lead. A chop of steel, a spray of blood. A turbaned head rolling across the deck.

I bellowed, charging a soldier who aimed his musket at Caesar's back. *No one kills Caesar!* The soldier faltered, and I swung at his head with my cutlass. He parried with the barrel of his musket. Metal jarred against metal. Back I slashed. In an instant he dropped his musket and drew his cutlass. I stepped over the musket, pushing past a pirate who had stumbled to his knees, the hilt of a dagger protruding out of his belly. I pressed the soldier back, hacking, slashing. He lost his footing and fell back against a cannon. Then, with a practiced flick of my wrist, I sent his cutlass clattering to the deck.

In that instant I saw both surprise and terror in his eyes. A cry bubbled from deep within me, and I ran him through with my cutlass. The man stared at me, the surprise in his eyes dimming. I yanked my cutlass from his body and shoved him away with my foot.

For Timothy.

"Retreat!" I heard Josiah shout. "Retreat! There are too many of them! It's a trap!"

I stared at the man I'd just killed. He was young, maybe eighteen. My gorge rose, sour, burning. I leaned over and vomited.

My God, I'm a murderer. A killer.

With a cry of anguish, I fought my way toward Josiah's voice, stumbling over bodies, parrying blows on all sides with my cutlass. A soldier aimed his musket at my head, but I ducked as the gun fired, at the same time whipping my cutlass blade up, slicing his arm. He dropped his musket and grabbed his wound, mouth open in a scream. I left him there.

Retreat. Retreat.

Suddenly there was a sharp crack of timbers, and the deck

beneath me shuddered and heaved. I lost my balance and fell, at the same time trying to see what had happened. It was the *Defiance.* She had collided with the *Surat Merchant,* and now more pirates gushed aboard, surging like an ocean wave—a hundred more cutthroats, at least.

"Cease retreat!" commanded Josiah. "Stand and fight, men, fight! The *Defiance* is here! No quarter!"

The air renewed with the retort of musket and pistol fire, the clash of cutlasses, battle cries, explosions.

As I struggled to my knees, something ripped through my left arm like a red-hot poker. A curse lodged in my throat. I looked down. Blood poured from a wound in the fleshy part of my upper arm.

I've been shot!

Suddenly, out of the chaos, a soldier hurtled toward me, brandishing his cutlass, mouth open, screaming, eyes afire with murder. My vision narrowed, and I saw him as if from a distance, as if through a tunnel—he at one end, and I at the other—as if this weren't real. I dropped my cutlass, yanked out my pistol, and fired at his thigh, scarcely aware of him falling forward just inches from me, his cutlass flying useless into the air. He lay on his stomach, then raised himself and looked at me, his eyes filled with the expectation that I would kill him. But I could not. Would not.

Never again.

Tossing my pistol away and picking up my cutlass, eyes watering from the sulfurous stink, I stood and ran, tramping over bodies. Hands reached out, clutching my pant legs, my ankles. Someone pleaded, "Help me."

"Daniel! Over here!" I heard Josiah yell.

"I'm here!" I cried.

I'd lost my bearings, not knowing which way was forward or

aft, Josiah's voice seeming like it was coming from everywhere. From nowhere.

Then, suddenly, an explosion. I hurtled through the air, a wave of heat blasting over me. I tumbled hard against a bulkhead. *My arm! My arm!* I lay for a moment, blinking back the pain, wishing this wasn't real, not wanting to die. My eyes stung, and I tasted blood and smoke. Orange flame hissed and roared.

We're on fire. The Surat Merchant *is on fire!*

Smoke billowed upward, blocking out the sun. I staggered to my feet, groaning, aching. Blood seeped into my eyes from a cut on my forehead. Already my kerchief was soaked through. "Josiah!" I shouted.

But there was no answer.

Instead, to my horror, Gideon Fist stepped out of the swirling smoke. Like the devil come straight from the bowels of the earth.

CHAPTER 18

*B*lackened by soot, he clutched a cutlass in one hand, a pistol in the other.

Except for his crossbelt holding two brace of pistols, Fist was bare-chested, hairy, shining with sweat, the bullet wound on his belly puckered and purple. He was breathing hard, his chest heaving. His red beard appeared to be on fire. Smoke rose from its curling depths, seeping about his head, swirling to his eyes, red-rimmed and murderous and looking right at me.

All pain suddenly forgotten, I whipped out my dagger from behind my back and threw it in one motion. He dodged to the side, the dagger sailing past him into the smoke.

Fist smiled. "Well, what do you know. It's the puppy."

Frantic, I searched about for my cutlass, having lost it in the explosion. A dead man lay near me, bloody fingers curled about a cutlass. I snatched it up and whirled, facing Fist.

He advanced. Fire roared behind him. I had nowhere to go; the bulkhead pressed against my back. I moved sideways over bodies, trying to find some space behind me.

Suddenly, with a roar like a beast from hell, he rushed forward, and in five steps he was upon me. But, to my surprise, he did not shoot me or thrust at me with his cutlass, instead only beating aside my attempts to skewer him. All defense.

Of course. He wants you alive. Dead, you are of no worth to him.

I bellowed, renewing my efforts. I slashed at him from above, from below, dagger now in my left hand, both weapons moving, slashing, hacking, thrusting, trying every trick I'd ever learned. But he was powerful. A devil, indeed, warding off each stroke like he was made of stone, not flesh.

And then he whipped me with the flat of his cutlass directly on my bullet wound. Pain and nausea washed over me. My vision wavered. I cried out. Dropped my dagger. Stumbled over a body. And in that moment, Fist swung back and hit me aside the head with the butt of his pistol.

Stars exploded, shooting across the sky of my mind before everything went black.

I awoke to the stench of body odor. Candle smoke. Dampness. Mildew.

It was stiflingly hot. My arm burned with fire, and I couldn't remember why it hurt so. I tried to move away from the pain, but it seemed to follow me.

I heard water sloshing, a shout from far away, the groan of timbers, a low chuckle—menacing and near.

Where am I? What has happened?

I opened my eyes, slowly, a crack only, wincing. Pain stabbed my temples.

I lay in a bed. Fist sat in a chair beside me. Seeing him, my memory returned: the battle, the soldiers, my wounds, the explosions, my fight with Fist, getting hit over the head with a pistol butt. And now? Now I was certain that I was aboard the *Defiance,* in the captain's cabin, lying atop Fist's own bed that smelled of rats' nests and stale sweat.

With a startled cry, I sat up, trying to reach for my weapon, any weapon. But I discovered my wrists were bound to the wood rails on the sides of the bed. I was trapped.

"Looking for these?" Fist asked, gesturing toward a table. Upon it lay my three remaining pistols and a dagger.

I groaned and lay back down, head swirling. "Josiah will find me," I managed to say.

At this, Fist grinned broadly. "Your beloved Captain Black is dead. Burnt to a crisp."

I blinked at him, wondering. *Is it true?* "You're a liar."

Fist's eyes narrowed and darkened, and his smile abruptly ceased.

I shrank back against the straw mattress.

He thrust his face into mine. His beard tickled my skin. His breath stank of decay. "There is only one thing I want from you, puppy. Can you guess what it is?"

No doubt Fist had already searched me for the map but had missed it, scrawled as it was on the underside of my crossbelt.

Is Josiah really dead?

"I know what it is you want," I retorted, trying to hide the quiver of my lip. "You need me to teach you how to fight with a cutlass. You're not very quick and you tire easily."

Fist's eyes flashed with anger. "Wrong answer." And so saying, he ground the butt of his pistol directly into the wound in my arm.

I threw my head back and screamed.

He stopped after a while. I lay panting, sweat trickling off me, heart hammering from the shock of pain.

"Don't be a fool, boy. Tell me where you hid the treasure."

"What—what treasure?"

Again the pistol butt ground in the wound, harder this time. I gritted my teeth. Nausea bubbled. *Merciful God. How much longer can I take this?*

It would be simpler to just give him the map. But then he would merely kill me.

No, I had to endure. I couldn't tell him—not if I wished to live.

Once again he stopped. "Now, my good sense tells me that you're a clever lad. You've got that gleam of intelligence in your eye. And you're smart enough to figure that this pains you more than it pains me. Just tell me where the treasure is, and I promise to let you go. You'll never have to hurt again."

"How many times do I have to tell you?" I gasped. "You're— you're a liar."

I was immediately sorry for the rashness of my words, for he roared a thunderous roar, eyes bulging. He stood, his chair crashing to the floor, and grabbed my dagger from atop the table. The blade glinted in the feeble candlelight.

My heart crashed against my ribs. *What is he going to do?*

In two seconds, I had my answer.

He grabbed my left hand and held the dagger's blade over the top knuckle of my little finger. "Talk or I'll slice it off."

I started to squirm, trying to pull my hand away. "Help! Down here! I'm being held prisoner!" And that's when the dagger bit deep. Pressing down hard. Slicing. Severing tendons. Bone. Me, screaming. Screaming. *Oh, God. Help me!*

I thought of Faith. I thought of her and her child—my half brother or my half sister. I thought of them, destitute perhaps, hungry, alone. I remembered my promise to my father that I would care for Faith. And I could not do that if I was dead. I had to return to America, if only for her.

Even after Fist finished cutting off the first knuckle of my finger, rivers of pain continued to wash through me, searing me. Every muscle quivered. I rocked my head from side to side, crying hot tears. *Save me, Father!*

A hand grabbed my hair, yanked my face toward his. "Tell me," he snarled. "Or I'll cut you knuckle by knuckle until you're only good for fish food. Tell me!"

I blinked at him through a haze of tears. His eyes, filled with hate. His face, twisted with rage, blood spatters on his cheeks. Before I could stop myself, I gathered what saliva I could and spat in his face. "Clean yourself off."

I think I shrieked even louder this time, shrill and inhuman-sounding. I heard the crack of bone.

No!

No! . . .

Knuckle by knuckle . . . again . . . again . . .

A deep haze of pain covered me like a burial shroud when, suddenly, the door burst open. I was vaguely aware of someone drawing a cutlass, a roar of rage from Fist, a clash of steel.

I heard boots scuffling across the floor, furniture being thrown aside. Someone stumbled on top of me and then off again. The clash, clang, clash of steel. And finally a cry of death, choked, surprised. Then silence.

Silence . . .

Then he was untying my bonds. I groaned. He lifted me out

of the bed, saying, "I've got you now, Daniel, my boy. You're safe. No one's going to hurt you ever again."

And he carried me away, onto the open deck, fresh air in my face, the dampness of my tears cool upon my cheeks. My head sagged. I closed my eyes. Heard the beat of his heart.

It was as if I were four years old again. A boy. Clasped tight in Josiah's arms. Breathing in the scent of rum and tobacco.

My favorite smell . . .

CHAPTER 19

$\mathcal{W}$e lost twenty-two men.

Lost the *Surat Merchant* and her cargo as well. For she had burned, an inferno, flames snapping taller than the highest mast, until she sank from sight, a steaming hiss of bubbles.

With the death of Fist, the men of the *Defiance* had quickly regrouped and voted their quartermaster as captain. Josiah continued as commander of the fleet. The men of the *Defiance* and the *Sweet Jamaica* were getting desperate, however, for since they had not participated in the capture of the first merchant ship, they had as yet received no prize.

After a half day spent licking their wounds, the three pirate ships chased down and successfully plundered two more ships of the pilgrim fleet, taking more than ten days to do so. Fortunately, neither of the ships was filled with soldiers, as the *Surat Merchant* had been. Instead, like the *Jedda,* they were filled with wealthy passengers and enough booty to make every pirate giddy with dreams of the easy life.

All this I learned later, for I was incapacitated in Josiah's cabin, shivering with fever, frozen to my marrow though the air dripped with heat and moisture. My left hand and arm swelled, turning an angry red. Foul liquid seeped from the wounds.

I vaguely remember an Indian woman coming into the cabin. Stooped, wrinkled, and brown. Silks swishing. Brushing away the flies from around my face. I remember the smell of heated herbs, her making me drink something bitter, hot bandages upon my wounds, steaming hot, but still a relief—blessed relief. I loosened my tongue enough to thank her. Told Josiah to give her half my share, that she was a good woman. At least that's what I think I said, for I mumbled, tongue thick as paste, and could scarce remember who I was from one moment to the next.

I don't know how many days passed before I finally awakened, my head clear.

I was alone in Josiah's cabin. It was daytime and, judging from the sounds and the heel of the ship, the *Tempest Galley* was under sail, moving fast.

My left hand and upper arm were swathed in bandages. Another bandage wrapped around my head, covering the gash on my forehead. I tossed aside the thin covering and sat up. Immediately the room spun in a dizzy whirl, and I fell back heavily on the bed, realizing at the same time that my body was dressed in nothing but a silk banyan.

Slowly, Daniel, slowly, I told myself.

I sat up again, gritting my teeth. Feet dangling, head pounding, I hesitated only a moment before unwrapping the bandage covering my hand, dreading what I would find.

A cry escaped my mouth. *My God! I'm mutilated!* My little finger and the finger next to it had been sliced off down to the base knuckle. Only two fingers and a thumb were left. The wounds were pink, slightly swollen, crusted over. I sat for a while staring at my hand, horrified, flies buzzing around me. Finally, carefully, I moved my hand, biting my lip against the pain. I made a fist, flexed the remaining fingers, open, closed. *It's ugly, but it moves. It works.*

Surprising myself, I smiled, thinking, *It's better than being dead.*

And with that thought, my stomach growled, and I realized I was ravenously hungry.

I rewrapped the bandage and stood, hugging the walls, the furniture. Out I staggered onto the upper deck, the sun piercing the backs of my eyes like a hot iron. I blinked, only then becoming aware that everyone was staring at me. Josiah climbed down the fo'c'sle companionway and strode across the upper deck toward me. He was smiling, his eyes bright. "Daniel! You're up!"

I fought the urge to embrace him. Instead, I said in a voice cracked with disuse, "I'm hungry."

"Is that all you have to say after two weeks of lying about like a prince and doing nothing? Cook! A bit of service here, if you please! Prince Daniel desires some food lest he wither and perish. And some fresh clothes too, you lazy lot of scoundrels! Look lively now!"

"Aye, Captain!" Abe hollered from where he stood beside the giant pots, located in the open area beneath the fo'c'sle deck. "A feast of all feasts coming right up! A prince's delight! We'll have that boy climbing the shrouds faster than you can whistle!"

And to my surprise, Caesar sprang to his feet and returned momentarily with my clothes, freshly washed and folded and smelling somewhat clean—comparatively speaking, of course. "Josiah say you save my life, Fat Boy." Caesar grinned, handing me my clothing. "Caesar say thank you."

I stammered out my thanks, confused and embarrassed by the royal treatment.

Each limb trembled as though I was a babe just learning to walk. My heart raced and skittered. My head started to throb. I needed to go back and rest.

Josiah must have read my thoughts, for he ushered me into his cabin and helped me dress. *Like a father with a young child,* I thought.

By the time I was clothed, Abe entered and set a bowl of food on the table. "Careful you don't burn your mouth now. It's hotter than Hades. Don't overeat either—you've been sick, you know. We've all been praying for your recovery. Much as pirates pray, that is, and much as the good Lord is willing to listen to hellbound rascals such as us."

"Thanks," I said, seating myself at the table. Abe left the cabin, closing the door behind him.

The stew was delicious—a spicy mixture of fish, eggs, chicken, olives, garlic, oil, palm hearts, and turtle meat. But after just a few mouthfuls, I was already full, disappointingly full. I took one last bite and pushed the bowl away. Only then did I realize that Josiah sat opposite me, smoking his long pipe, watching me.

With a creak of rigging and timbers, the ship increased her heel. My bowl of stew and the goblet slid across the table, the bowl stopped from falling over the edge by the table runners, the goblet stopped when Josiah wrapped his long fingers around it.

"Tell me what this is," he said, his voice sounding like I'd always remembered it, silken. He slid my leather crossbelt, underside up, across the table toward me.

I swallowed my food with a gulp. Quick as a wink, I snatched up the belt, slipped it over my shoulder, and buckled it across my chest. "Nothing. Just my crossbelt."

For a while Josiah was silent, seemingly content just to watch me. I grew uncomfortable under his gaze. *Did he guess? Does he know it's a map? Does he know I hoard a treasure that I refuse to share? A treasure that I plan for good, not ill?*

The corners of Josiah's mouth hinted of a smile. "Anyone knows that the first order of business when torturing someone for information is to check their person thoroughly. But then, Fist always was more brute than brains."

He knows! Josiah knows it's a map!

He continued, "The men think you killed him."

"What?" My jaw dropped with surprise. *Me? Kill Fist?*

Josiah shrugged. "I saw no reason to tell them otherwise. Let them think you can beat the best of them. It will make you safer in the long run. And now you are no longer a boy in their eyes. You are a man."

I glanced at my hand, bulky with bandages. I wondered what would happen to me now that I had only eight fingers.

Josiah stood. "Get some rest, Daniel. You're looking pale and none too steady." He walked to the door.

But there was something burning inside me. Something that had been nagging me upon awakening. "Josiah?"

"Yes?" He turned, hand on the latch.

"Thank you." When he said nothing, I continued. "Thank you for saving me."

Josiah blinked as if surprised. "You're welcome." Again he turned to go.

"Josiah?"

"Yes?"

"Why? Why did you do it? Why did you save me? You have always protected me. Why?"

Josiah paused, seeming to think, searching my eyes all the while. Finally he said, "I can't explain it. Not yet anyway. Perhaps someday I will."

"Josiah?"

"Yes?"

"Please don't take this the wrong way. But—but I must still see you hang for your crime. It is my duty. As a good son. You understand that, don't you? You have saved my life, but the life of my father is still forfeit. Please understand, please. It is what any good son must do."

Again Josiah blinked. "Get some rest," was all he said. And he left, closing the door softly behind him.

For the rest of the day I cried miserably. *Wasn't that what I was supposed to say? Am I not a good son? A son who witnessed his father slain for the sake of honor? Where is my honor? My father's honor? Am I not a good son?*

When darkness came, I finally fell asleep. Yet my sleep was tormented, tossed with unsettled dreams.

Timothy, holding his innards.

Pirates dangling. Jerking. Struggling to breathe. Faces turning purple. Hemp digging deep.

Faith patting my head, her face shrunken and starved, a babe in her arms—a tiny shriveled skeleton.

My father, arms outstretched, palms upward, pleading, *Forgive, Daniel. There has been enough bloodshed.*

Forgive . . .

CHAPTER 20

$\mathcal{W}$e were headed back to Madagascar, to the island of Saint Mary's.

My plan was simple. While we careened the ships, relaxed in the sun, enjoyed the bounty of the island's foods, I would fetch my treasure, bringing it aboard a little at a time so as not to attract undue attention. I would stow it away in a secret place I had secured, deep in the shot locker. And when we returned to America, I would be free to go my way, as would any pirate who wished to do so, our contract with one another complete.

Whether I would bring Josiah to justice for the murder of my father, I admit I no longer knew, despite what I'd told Josiah. I prayed to God for guidance, but, like so many times before, God was silent on that account. Josiah had saved my life, yet he had murdered my father. As my father's son, I was duty-bound to seek revenge, to demand justice. Was I not?

I was beginning to realize that revenge was a burden—a terrible, terrible burden that gnawed my insides relentlessly. I wanted to be rid of it, yet how could I forgive the murderer of my father?

Even though it had been a week since my recovery, I had yet to move out of Josiah's cabin. Instead, Josiah strung a hammock in the corner and slept there while I still slept in his bed. I awoke many nights screaming, dreaming of turbaned heads rolling across a deck, of a man staring at me as I ran him through with my cutlass, of blood sprayed through the air like mist, of Fist standing in fire and brimstone, of Josiah dangling from a noose, face blue, neck askew.

"Daniel, my boy! 'Tis a nightmare. Just a dream!" And he would shake me awake as my cries faded away.

One night, I bolted upright in bed, sweating, heart pounding, the hair on my arm raised in gooseflesh as the echo of my shriek faded throughout the ship. *Dear God!* Now there was nothing but the gentle sloshing of the water on the ship's hull, the familiar creak of timbers, the squawk of a parrot overhead—a pet of one of the pirates.

"Daniel?"

"Aye."

"Are you all right, my boy?"

The nightmare lingered like a foul stench, wretched and sickening. . . . "He was cutting them off, one by one. I couldn't stop him. I kept calling for you but you were dead. . . . He told me you were dead. I—I—" My voice faded away, and I sank back into the mattress, shuddering, remembering.

After a while, I heard Josiah get out of his hammock and

fumble in the darkness. A flame flared as he lit the overhead lantern. Weak light now filtered through the cabin, casting deep shadows. Josiah shut the lantern casing and looked at me, his face shadowed. "There's something I must tell you." So saying, he poured two goblets of wine and set them on the table, hands trembling. I was astonished. I'd never seen his hands tremble before.

Crawling out of bed, I sat on the chair and drank deeply of the wine.

After fiddling again with the lantern, after topping off my goblet with more wine, after tying back his hair, which had become tousled in the night, and lighting his long pipe, Josiah sat across from me. I could see his eyes now, liquid black in the dim light. They were troubled . . . afraid, even.

Afraid? Captain Josiah Black—the most sought-after cutthroat in the world—afraid? An unsettling feeling crept over me, that long-ago feeling that my life was about to change. My breathing quickened. I was uncertain if I wanted to hear what he had to say, yet I knew I had to.

He ran his tongue across his lips and cleared his throat. "Daniel . . ."

"Aye. I'm listening."

"There's something you need to know. Something I should have told you long ago."

Josiah seemed to struggle with the words. He took a drink of wine, wiping his mouth with his sleeve.

"When I was a younger man, I was—I was in love."

I stayed silent. My hand throbbed and my stomach growled. I was hungry again.

"She—she was beautiful. Young like me. We were fools, she and I. Fools in love. We thought the world would part before us, like Moses parting the Red Sea. We thought nothing could stop two people so deeply in love." He snorted, a laugh of derision. "But the world does not suffer fools gladly." Josiah gazed at me, as if begging me to understand. "I was a privateer at that time, living in Boston—you do know what a privateer is, don't you?"

I nodded. A privateer was issued a letter of marque from the government that authorized him to raid and plunder the ships of enemy nations. It was like being a pirate, except it was a legal and acceptable method of war.

"I was commissioned as a privateer by one of the colonial governors. Given the finest ship in the fleet." Here Josiah hesitated, then looked away. "But, unknown to the governor, the woman whom I loved was his daughter—his only daughter."

"So what happened?" I asked, leaning forward.

Smoke from the long pipe swirled about Josiah, rising in slow curls. "I went away on a privateering voyage. A very successful one, I might add. In the interim, unknown to me, several things happened."

"What things?"

"First, she discovered she was with child. My child. Second, her father learned of our clandestine relationship and forbade her ever to see me again, calling me a bloody scoundrel, a Judas, a philanderer, and things much worse than that."

"And?"

"In outrage and in a desperate attempt to salvage his daughter's honor, he quickly arranged a marriage with one of the town's leading citizens. A merchant."

I swallowed hard. Part of me wanted him to continue. Part of me wanted him to stop, to not say another word. Not now. Not ever. "Go on," I said, my voice a whisper.

"So, within a month of my leaving on my privateering voyage, while I was still dreaming of the day we could be together forever as husband and wife, they were married. Her merchant husband was never the wiser, raising the child as his own, always believing the child was his."

Josiah stopped and looked full at me.

I could no longer meet his gaze. Tears filled my eyes. The goblet shimmered in the lantern light. When I took a drink, it was my hand that now shook.

"When I returned from my voyage, the governor declared me an outlaw. A pirate. Denied that he'd ever signed a letter of marque on my behalf. And for the life of me, I could not find the letter. Likely he had one of his cronies steal it." His fingers whitened as he squeezed the goblet. I saw rage in his eyes—a long ago, hurt-filled rage. "He confiscated all the goods I had obtained and threw me into prison to await trial. But I escaped."

"What then?"

"I was furious, of course. I commandeered my former privateering vessel, renamed her the *Tempest Galley,* and proclaimed myself a pirate. My first order of business was to plunder and burn every ship the governor owned. I ruined him, Daniel. Ruined him utterly. He died not long after. And there's been a price on my head ever since."

For a while I was silent, scarce able to comprehend what I was hearing. "And what of—what of the child?"

Josiah regarded me, saying nothing.

"Then at least tell me her name." Again, silence. "Pray tell me. What was her name? The one that you loved?"

Instead of answering, Josiah pushed back his chair and crossed the room. He rifled through a drawer at the captain's desk, finally withdrawing a folded letter. For a while he stood fingering the letter, as if deliberating whether or not to give it to me. Finally he sat down again and handed me the letter. The parchment was thin, yellowed, dry, the edges ragged and grayed as if it had been handled a hundred times, a thousand times. Yet the green wax seal was still intact.

Written on the outside of the letter was a single name: *Daniel.*

Josiah spoke. "Her name was Abigail Ball Markham."

CHAPTER 21

My dearest Daniel,

The doctor tells me I have not much longer to live—a day, perhaps. I am weak and feverish, and it is difficult to write a letter of such proportions, but I feel a weight upon my soul to tell you the truth. I pray that someday you will read this letter and find it in your heart to forgive me. Perhaps once you know the truth, I will be able to rest in eternal peace, absolved from any deception.

Before I loved your father, or rather, before I loved Robert Markham, I loved another man. We planned to be married, but he embarked upon a privateering voyage before that could be accomplished. Finding myself with child and unwed, I went to my father, who quickly arranged a marriage with a very fine man, one whom I have learned to love deeply. Of all things, Daniel, you must at least believe that. I love Robert Markham deeply. To this day, Robert believes you are his natural son. I have never told him the truth, and forbear to do so, as I believe it would devastate him, for he indeed loves you as a father loves his son.

Pray forgive me, Daniel, for any pain I have caused you with this revelation. Pray forgive me so that I might rest in eternal peace, for I go to my grave with my heart heavy and filled with unresolved anguish. Please know that I have loved you always and will love you forever. This evening I had you brought to me and gave you my miniature in a locket. May you treasure it always as a token of my love for you, my son.

I send this letter with a trusted servant to be delivered this night to your natural father. He will keep it with the understanding to give it to you at a time in your life when and if it is appropriate. Despite what your natural father has become, and despite the pain he caused both me and my father, understand that I forgive him and love him still. Things could have been so different, but alas, we are given but one pass through life, and mine has come to a close.

May God bless you. May you abide in happiness, and may your life be filled with goodness and charity, as befitting all of God's children. Until we greet one another in the realm of eternal glory, I remain always and forever,

Your loving mother,
Abigail Markham

The letter slipped to my lap. Smudges of ink. Swirls of black.

I buried my head in my arms, all the anguish I'd ever felt gushing out in a torrent.

Mother. My mother. How I have longed to hear your voice again.

I fumbled for the locket and clutched it in my hand, wishing I could feel her touch just once more, wishing she had never died, wishing everything could be the way it used to be, wishing I did not know what I knew now.

Father, you will always be my father. Nothing can take away what we had together. Nothing.

After a while a hand pressed my shoulder—not the ethereal hand of an angelic being, but a hand of flesh and bone. I raised my head. Josiah gave me a handkerchief. I wiped my eyes and blew my nose.

I couldn't look him in the eye. Now I knew why he had always protected me, why he had always shown me kindness.

"All this time you have known," I whispered.

"Aye."

I heard the creak of his chair as he seated himself across from me once again.

Thoughts rushed in and out, caught in a hurricane, leaving me tossed, ripped open, laid bare. Questions jumbled over one another until they spilled out like blood pouring from a wound. "When did you start to have business dealings with my father?"

"Soon after your mother died."

"Why not earlier?"

"She did not approve. She knew what I had become, and she was angry because of what I'd done to your grandfather."

"But after she died you approached my father."

"Aye. To be near you."

"And my father never knew?"

"Never."

"And then you betrayed him."

Josiah paused. "He betrayed me, Daniel. He betrayed all of us, the same way your grandfather betrayed me."

Tears welled in my eyes. "But you killed the one man who acted as a father to me for all my life, who *was* a father to me."

He said nothing.

"Who else knows about this? About you being my—being my—" I could not say the word.

"Only Basil Higgins. He's been with me from the beginning."

I thought back, remembering. "Would you—would you really have left me upon that deserted island with nothing but a barrel of biscuit and a pistol?"

"Yes, but I never would have left you alone. I would have stayed with you. You must trust me, Daniel—I have never wanted to see you hurt. I would rather give up all the fortune in the world than to lose you a second time. What happened once will not happen again."

"Why haven't you told me any of this before now?"

"You would not have listened."

Now I stared at him, my lips quivering, seeing him through a haze of tears as if for the first time. An awkwardness stood between us. I still held my mother's locket. "So what happens now?"

"I do not know, Daniel, my boy."

Come the first light of dawn, I moved out of Josiah's cabin.

"Lovers' quarrel?" someone asked, giggling like a girl, his teeth glinting gold in the sunrise.

Before I could stop myself, I punched him as hard as I could in the gut and walked away, finding no pleasure in hearing him grunt and gasp for breath. I half expected him to come after me, to challenge me to a duel. But he didn't, my reputation for killing Fist likely staying his hand.

I settled beside the fo'c'sle rail, squeezing between two snoring pirates, welcoming the breeze, watching the sun rise.

Once again my world had been shattered. A thousand million thoughts and feelings ate away at me, like woodworm eating the ship's timbers. It was too much, too much.

I pressed my hands against the sides of my head as if trying to contain my thoughts, to control them, to piece back together the fragments of my shattered life.

What am I to do now? What about my father? What about Josiah? Has my whole life been a lie? Has everyone I have ever loved deceived me?

Just get the treasure, I firmly told myself. *Get the treasure. Beyond that, I cannot think.*

"You're back," said Josiah. He stood in the doorway of his cabin, sunlight streaming from behind him.

I returned to my task of searching under his bed. "Just came to fetch my other stockings. The ones I'm wearing are full of holes. Rats chewed on them last night, I think." I fumbled through the dust, the discarded clothes, crumpled papers, a forgotten goblet, aware he was watching me, wondering what he was thinking, wishing he would say something . . . anything.

Then I heard him moving behind me, a drawer opening. "Here, take these." He held out several pairs of his stockings.

I hesitated before standing and selecting a pair. "Thanks. That's all I need."

He shrugged as if it made no difference to him and placed the rest back in the drawer and closed it, his back turned toward me.

I stood awkwardly with my one pair of stockings, knowing I should leave.

Words rushed to my mouth. *I wish you would have told me earlier. Don't you see how everything has changed? Are you truly my father? Did you know my mother still loved you, even after what you had done?* But instead of speaking, I stared at a frayed hole in the elbow of his sleeve, at his rigid shoulders, at his dagger sheathed at the small of his back.

The silence deepened until I could stand it no more.

I turned and walked through the open doorway into the sunshine, blinking from the brightness.

Josiah said, "Daniel—"

My heart skipped. "Yes?"

But to my disappointment, all he said was, "Don't forget your Bible." He was standing in the darkness of the cabin, holding out the book, his eyes masked. "You left it on the bed."

"Oh. Thanks."

I took the Bible and left.

Off the coast of Saint Mary's, a longboat filled with twenty men approached, single sail white against the turquoise-blue waters. We neared the bottleneck harbor where we had careened our ship and taken on provisions last spring, near where my treasure was buried. We did not know who the people in the longboat were, but we hove to and waited alongside the *Defiance* and the *Sweet Jamaica*.

It was early November, and we were all anxious to make landfall, for it had been seven months since we'd left Saint Mary's, the only landfall since then being the rock-strewn, ovenbaked, waterless island in the Red Sea.

I was especially anxious, for I could scarce wait to fetch my treasure.

Once within hailing distance, one of the longboat's men stood and shouted, "Where are you from?"

To which Josiah replied, "From the sea," the universal code of the brotherhood.

"Likewise!"

Soon they were aboard, introducing themselves all around, asking for food and drink, of which we had plenty, having forcibly acquired much of it from the ships of the pilgrim fleet, in addition to all manner of sailing gear and essentials.

When they were finally seated about the mainmast, wooden bowls in hand, Josiah asked them their business.

"Come to warn you," said the leader, his mouth filled with stew. "Don't enter the harbor."

"And why not?" asked Josiah.

The leader, whose name was Curly George, chewed and swallowed noisily. "Malagasy rose up and murdered a bunch of pirates. Slit their throats, quiet as you please. We only just managed to get away. But our boat's leaky as a sieve, eaten by worm. So we've been stuck here, unable to sail more than here and there."

News of the rebellion caused a murmur to ripple through the pirates, pressed about the new men like moths gathered about a lantern.

"Why did the Malagasy rebel?" asked Josiah.

Curly George gulped his wine, wiped his face on his hairy arm, and belched. "Merchant vessels arrive all the time laden with goods for the pirates. The vessels always leave with a cargo of slaves. African slaves mostly, captured by the Malagasy for trade. It's a handy arrangement all the way around."

"So what happened?"

"Well, this time there weren't enough slaves, so the fellow in the fort got greedy and tricked a bunch of Malagasy into coming aboard the merchant vessel. Clapped 'em in irons, and that was that—they was slaves. 'Course, that didn't hold too well with the rest of the Malagasy. Pirates had always treated them fair. Partners in trade and marriage and all of that. Anyway, Saint Mary's is too hot to handle right now, and my boys and I need safe passage. We'll be glad to join your fine crew if you can spare the room."

Of course there was a general hubbub, men murmuring among one another, some cursing their rotten luck. A general council was called. With the raising of the green silk flag, the crews from the two other ships came aboard the *Tempest Galley.*

"Sail into the harbor anyway," some said. "Blow the Malagasy to hell."

"Even if we do blow the Malagasy to hell," others said, "there will be no provisions with which to resupply. We must find another anchorage."

It was debated, argued, debated, and finally voted upon.

The men of the *Sweet Jamaica* and the *Defiance* would take their share of the treasure and head to Cochin, India, off again on their own account, fencing their goods to eager Indian merchants and then heading back to the Red Sea for another year of plunder. They hadn't earned as much as the men aboard the *Tempest Galley* and wouldn't quit until they were satisfied.

Those aboard the *Tempest Galley,* plus the new men, would sail nine hundred miles to Saint Augustine's Bay on the western side of Madagascar, where the natives were friendly to pirates, where we could careen our ship and resupply in preparation for the long voyage to the colonies.

Leaving my treasure behind.

CHAPTER 22

The days were long and brutally hot, and I'd lost my desire for swordplay. I missed Timothy, miscreant though he was. I missed my father, my mother. I missed Boston.

I had decided. I would *not* see Josiah hang, seeing as he was my natural father. Such a decision, hard-wrought and wrested after many sleepless nights, gave me enormous relief, as if I'd thrown off a millstone that had been crushing me with its weight.

I tried to tell Josiah this one day, to tell him that I had come to a decision. I hesitated before rapping on his cabin door, and when he said, "Come!" I entered. He was sitting at his desk, studying his charts. "Yes?" he said, only glancing up briefly.

Again, the familiar awkwardness stood

between us, so thick now I could have stabbed it with my dagger. "I've come to tell you that I've decided not to seek justice concerning my father. I—I no longer wish to see you hang."

For a long time he said nothing, making notations upon a chart, his face expressionless. I heard the creak of his chair, a burst of drunken laughter overhead, the squawk of a chicken. "Is that all?"

A heaviness settled in my chest, raw and aching. "Aye." And when he continued studying his charts, seeming to take no notice of me, I left. *Does he no longer care for me?* I wondered that night as I lay in my hammock. *Or did he only pretend to care so that I would absolve him of his guilt?*

We no longer talked to each other, Josiah and I. I scarce looked his way whenever he came around, the awkwardness continuing to grow until it seemed as impenetrable as brick. For his part, he kept aloof from both me and the crew—a lone figure on the poop deck, taking the noon sighting, or fetching his food from Abe. And other than to order a sail loosed or reefed or to call out a new course, he hardly uttered a word.

Upon leaving Saint Augustine's Bay come the new year, the *Tempest Galley* clean once again and filled with fresh water and foodstuffs, half the crew became ill with jungle fever. It was a nasty fever, liquefying the bowels so that at any one time, at least a dozen men perched on the bowsprit, groaning, relieving themselves with a sickening stench into the waters below. Even Josiah was hit with the fever, and it was an odd thing to see my proud captain father aching and groaning along with the rest of them.

As for me, I moved my bedding amidships, between two cannon, away from the stench. I had remained surprisingly healthy, helping the others occasionally by giving them water, feeding those who were too weak to do so themselves. Of course I took on more than my fair share of ship's duties, but now I was eager to be home and did it of necessity.

By the time the *Tempest Galley* rounded the Cape of Good Hope, heading into the Atlantic, the fever finished wreaking its havoc. Thirty-six men had perished, including Will Putt. We saw several merchant ships but forbore attacking them, as we were too weak to manage it.

My bandages had come off long ago. My upper arm was fine, the skin pink and puckered around the old bullet wound. And though my hand was mutilated, I'd learned to use it well and had lost but little strength. The scar on my forehead was about two inches long, indented as though I'd been chopped with a hatchet. But, like the other wounds, it had healed cleanly. I silently thanked the Indian woman, knowing she had done me a great service. She had had no reason to help me—her ship was being plundered even as she ministered to my wounds. Such kindness touched me deeply.

May your life be filled with goodness and charity, my mother had written.

It made me wonder.

I had decided that once I arrived in the colonies, I would find Faith and care for her and her child, as I had originally promised. It was my last act of love for the man who had loved me as his son. This, not vengeance, would be my debt to my father. I had also decided that I was finished with this life at sea, this life of ill-adventure. Though my natural father was a pirate, *I* was *not* a pirate, nor would I ever be. I only wanted home. Especially since it was clear that, following his confession, Josiah no longer cared for me.

In anticipation of arriving at the colonies, I exchanged a ruby for a long, heavy coat. Basil thought me crazy, as coats weren't worth as much as rubies. Come evenings, I sat between the two cannon with a needle and thread. I detached the coat's lining and sewed in a layer of coins and jewel-filled bags—my share of the booty. Strange coins printed with strange letterings—gold, silver, big, little, square, round, stamped with crowns, heads of kings and emperors. I had used most of my coins to purchase more jewels, as jewels were easier to conceal and not as heavy.

One evening at twilight, Basil came and sat astride one of the cannon. "Ah," he said, "I see you're planning for the future. Anyone with half an eye can tell you're a smart lad. How old are you now? Sixteen?"

I nodded and tied off a knot, biting the thread with my teeth.

Basil waited for a while, then sighed. "May as well get straight to the point, seeing as you're not in a talkative mood. Josiah told me that he told ye all about it."

"He *what?*"

"Now, don't be getting all stirred up. I'm just saying that I know that ye know, that's all." He peered around secretively. "And don't ye be worrying yourself at all about anyone else knowing, because I can keep my lips shut. Ye can attest to that."

I threaded my needle, wondering what it was he had come to tell me.

"Daniel—I don't know how to say this . . . oh, bloody fire, I might as well just come out and say it. Your father loves ye. There. I've said it."

I picked up an emerald, examining it in the twilight.

Basil coughed into his hand and continued. "What happened to him long ago wasn't fair. It wasn't his fault that the woman he loved and his only son were taken from him and given to someone else. And if the governor had had his way, Josiah would have been tried for piracy and hanged like a chicken. He was in a bad spot and didn't have any choice about matters. A lesser man would have given up and let himself be hanged, but not Josiah. He found a way to be near ye in spite of all that had happened."

Basil paused before adding, "You're more like him than ye think ye are, lad."

I said nothing, stabbing the coat with my needle, angry at myself when tears stung my eyes. *We are nothing alike! Nothing! I do not murder my friends!*

"Well, if you're thinking about that other bit, I have something to say about that too, I do. Dispatching your foster father was a nasty piece of work there, no doubt about it. But it was a matter of honor, and it had to be done. Don't ye see, Daniel? Your father stabbed us in the back after we had treated him with nothing but honor and friendship. He brought it upon himself."

I had known for a long time that my merchant father was no saint, as Timothy had once said. I had indeed "smelled the stink." But I loved him nonetheless.

After enduring my silence for a while longer, Basil patted my shoulder and left. The night closed around me, and I could scarce see the coins anymore, or the small silk packets of jewels. I gazed at the sky, seeing the first star of the night appear.

You may have loved me once, Josiah Black, but it is clear you no longer do. It is clear you no longer wish to be my father. You are as finished with me as I am with you.

'Twas the nineteenth day of April. Gray, rain-swollen clouds hovered over the choppy Atlantic waters, and the air was chill. Come midmorning, our lookout descried a sail three points off the windward bow. Immediately the pirates set all sail and lay in a new course toward the unsuspecting ship, securing any exposed cannon with canvas tents lest the promised rain begin to fall.

I was disheartened by our decision to pursue the vessel, for we were only several hundred miles from Boston now. For weeks we'd sailed the dreary Atlantic, and the closer we came to home, the more anxious I became. Each day seemed to stretch, minutes turning to hours, until it lasted forever. Now we would spend an additional day or two pursuing the vessel, and perhaps another few days looting them.

Would I never return home? I was finished with this life and longed to escape at the first opportunity, to put my back to the *Tempest Galley* and lose myself in the waterfront docks at Boston Harbor.

The excitement aboard the *Tempest Galley* faded to puzzlement when our prey also plied on all sail and set an intercept course. The puzzlement quickly changed to alarm when Josiah, who had been peering through his eyeglass atop the foremast crosstrees, slid down a backstay and called for everyone to gather around. "Man-o'-war," he told us. "Forty guns at least, and judging from her lines, she'll be faster than smoke and oakum."

As he spoke, the skies opened and a great rain began to pour. Thunder rumbled.

Water sluiced off Josiah's cocked hat. "It is possible that news of our misdeeds has already been reported by the mogul's representatives to the British authorities. After all, we spent much time in Saint Augustine's Bay. Time enough for an East Indiaman to sail ahead of us." He peered out into the gray gloom. "We shall try to outrun them, but be prepared for battle, men, if it comes to that."

Lightning flashed, followed by a crack of thunder so sharp it rattled my bones. The wind gusted suddenly and the *Tempest Galley* groaned, increasing her heel.

"Captain Black," cried the lookout, "I've lost sight of them in the storm."

Josiah smiled grimly. "Maybe we can slip through the gauntlet after all. Alter course to west by northwest and prepare to take in sail."

Inch by sodden inch, flogged by yards of beating canvas, we took in sail while perched precariously atop the footropes. Afterward we cleared the decks for battle, trailing the pinnace to our stern by its painter, and prepared our big guns and our weapons. I was soaked through, shivering cold, and famished by the time we finished. As yet, there was no sign of the man-o'-war. Perhaps we had indeed given her the slip.

I crouched with many others in the sheltered area beneath the fo'c'sle deck, gobbling a quick meal of salt beef and biscuit, trying to keep my pistols dry.

The *Tempest Galley* heaved and pitched through the waves. The wind roared through the rigging. Lightning flashed every few seconds, illuminating my shipmates' faces—eerie and ghostlike. Water poured over the aft edge of the fo'c'sle deck. Some leaked between the deck boards and trickled onto our heads. No one spoke, for speech was next to impossible. And besides, I knew they were sobered. Should the man-o'-war find us, we stood no chance—every man aboard would be either blown out of the water or hanged for piracy.

As they ate their meal, men glanced about them, as if they could spy the man-o'-war from beneath the fo'c'sle deck. An hour later, men visibly began to relax. Some got out their pipes and smoked a bit. Others joined in a game of dice. Still others left for their watch, replaced by sodden, shivering men who gratefully accepted some salt beef and biscuit from Abe, tired though we all were of such miserable fare. One game fellow even tried to drown out the storm with his accordion.

As he was singing about the fine ladies of Port Royal—perfume, lace, and pretty smiles—we heard a cry from the lookout. A frightened shriek.

"Man-o'-war on our windward quarter! She's almost on us!"

For a split second, the men beneath the fo'c'sle deck stared at one another, faces deathly white with a stroke of lightning.

Then, like rats spilling out of a cellar, we tumbled over one another out onto the upper deck.

CHAPTER 23

$\mathcal{W}$ater, inches deep, rolled in waves across the upper deck, gurgling out the scuppers. I sloshed through it, rain spattering my face.

The man-o'-war was huge, ghostly, terrifying.

The very sight of her made my mouth dry.

Two decks of guns towering high.

A voice called from over the waters. "Strike! I order you to strike, in the name of His Britannic Majesty, King William of England!"

"We strike to no man!" cried Josiah.

There was a momentary pause before her cannon belched flame—a thunderous broadside aimed at us.

"Prepare to fire!" Josiah ducked as

cannonballs whizzed past, one mere inches from his head. "Cast loose the guns!"

This time the powder box was located on the lower deck, out of the rain. I scurried down and up the companionway, lungs burning, first wrapping each cartridge of gunpowder in a greased sailcloth to keep it dry.

Down in the lower deck, again and again, cannonballs smashed the hull of the *Tempest Galley*, sending a barrage of deadly splinters through the darkened corners.

On the upper deck, Josiah cried, "Fire!" And each time he cried thus, a boom loud as thunder exploded, the air convulsed with a shock wave, and the deck shivered beneath me. The two ships were now but one hundred feet apart, pummeling each other with shot as fast as the gunners could load and fire. I heard men screaming—shot with lead, pierced with wood shrapnel. One poor fellow was blasted into two parts, a twenty-four-pound cannonball through his middle.

I was on deck, running, cartridge tucked carefully to keep it dry.

"Worm and sponge!" Josiah was ordering.

As I passed, he grabbed my arm. "Take care, son," he said.

Startled, I looked him full in the face for the first time since the night of his confession. I wanted to tell him to have a care too, but my throat clogged and my tongue wouldn't work. Instead, I wrenched out of his grasp and was off and running again, slogging through the water, my heart twisting like a dagger inside my chest.

I handed over my cartridge to my gun crew, and after the powder and shot were rammed home, the guns of the *Tempest Galley* boomed once again.

Suddenly a great crack rent the air. There, across the water, the foremast of the man-o'-war began to teeter. Swaying for a moment as if undecided, the foremast finally fell, creaking and crashing, men scattering out of its way on the deck beneath. Rigging snapped and sails billowed upward in a great whoosh.

The pirates erupted into cheering. We'd disabled them!

"Cease firing!" cried Josiah once the cheering somewhat abated. His face was hard, his eyes dark as the storm clouds. "Man the sweeps! Let's put some distance between us. Fine work, men."

I hurried below—not to man the sweeps but to put on my coat, the one with my share of the loot sewn into the lining. I strapped my two daggers under my coat, plus a coil of rope, crossbelt secure as always across my chest. In addition, I stuffed the now flimsy and waterlogged document—the one declaring that I was a forced man, a hostage, with both Timothy and Abe's signatures as witnesses—into one of my pockets.

Back on the upper deck, I ran, long coat slapping my shins. By now the rain had stopped, the thunder a distant rumble. A gray mist had settled over the waters, the afternoon light fast fading.

I heard the sloshing of the sweeps in the water, felt the *Tempest Galley* gain speed. Josiah was amidships, talking with Basil. Glancing around to see if anyone had noticed me, I hurried into Josiah's cabin under the quarterdeck. I latched the door behind me, my breathing loud in my ears.

There wasn't much time.

Striding across the cabin, I flung open one of the stern windows and peered into the water below. The pinnace trailed behind the *Tempest Galley*, secured by a rope. She was half swamped—forgotten in the tumult of the storm and the battle.

Pulling out the rope from inside my coat, I secured one end to the bed railing and tossed the other out the window. I took a deep breath, said a quick prayer, climbed out the window, and slid down the rope, battered against the *Tempest Galley* as she heaved and tossed through the ocean swells. By the time I sat in the pinnace, water halfway to the thwarts, I was sore and bruised.

Just then, I saw movement up above. It was Josiah, leaning out the stern window. Our gazes locked.

Part of me wanted him to try to stop me, to plead with me not to leave. But he said nothing. His expression was unreadable, his eyes pools of black. Part of me wanted to stay, to stop myself from untying the pinnace, leaving the *Tempest Galley,* Josiah, and this life behind me.

But I untied the pinnace anyway, my hands shaking. I put the oars to the locks and began to row through the mist toward the man-o'-war. Again, my heart twisted, hurting. The pinnace rose heavily up and over the swells.

And Josiah grew smaller . . . smaller . . . framed like a miniature in the stern window until finally both he and the *Tempest Galley* disappeared in the mist.

I'm sure I made a sight—standing before the captain of the man-o'-war, damp and smelly as a bilge rat, a pool of water about my scruffy shoes, red kerchief wrapped round my head, skin darkened by sun and weather.

"They forced me to sign their Articles," I was telling him, "saying that unless I did they would maroon me on a deserted island. I was not a willing pirate."

"I see. And the name of the pirate captain?" Captain Wellington wore a powdered wig, tied in a queue beneath the cocked hat of a naval commander. Eyes pale as a morning sky pierced through me, as if he read my thoughts rather than heard my words.

"Josiah Sharp," I lied, hoping they would think he was just one of many petty pirates, rather than the most hunted cutthroat in the world.

Several of the captain's officers flanked him, and upon my words they glanced at one another as if they did not believe me. Immediately I sensed that something was wrong. The captain cocked his eyebrow. "And what waters did the *Tempest Galley* cruise?"

My heart began to pound. Was this a trap? Did they know something? "The—uh—the Red Sea. But we were unsuccessful." When the captain said nothing, I added, "I ask for safe passage to the colonies. As a forced man, I cannot be convicted of piracy. I have done nothing wrong." I cursed inwardly when my voice sounded unconvincing and weak.

"Tell me," said the captain, "how you came to be aboard the *Tempest Galley.*"

"They captured my father's ship."

"Ah. And your father's name?"

"Robert Markham. He was a merchant in Boston."

"I see. And your first name?"

"Daniel."

Upon my speaking such, the captain turned to his officers. "Bind him and throw him in the brig as a pirate."

The officers seized me. I heard a roar in my head. My temples pounded. *They're arresting me. Me! A forced man!* "But—but I told you that I was a forced man! You cannot do this!"

"We have orders to arrest one Daniel Markham on sight. This Daniel Markham will be aboard the *Tempest Galley,* having roamed the waters of the Red Sea and having participated in the capture and pillage of the merchant ship *Jedda,* among others." Again the eyes pierced me. "You are Daniel Markham, are you not?"

I was confused. How could they have possibly heard of me? "Yes, but I have done nothing wrong! Here, wait! I have the document to prove it." I tried to wrest out of their grasp, but they held me tight. "It's in my coat pocket. There. On the left."

The captain signaled one of the officers who stood beside me, pinning my arm. The officer reached in my coat pocket. A puzzled expression came over his face. He patted my coat, then opened it and in one motion, ripped off the lining. Gold and silver coins flashed in the lantern light. A silk packet of jewels dropped to the deck.

Silence pressed down.

The captain picked up the packet and with a tug opened it. He tapped the contents into his palm. Diamonds. Sparkling like ice.

The captain's voice was steely as a cutlass. "As I said, throw him in the brig. We'll return to Boston, where he'll stand trial for piracy. And may the Lord God have mercy on his soul."

CHAPTER 24

"*Set* the prisoner at the bar!"

The guards grabbed me and propelled me forward. Leg irons clanking, wrists manacled, I shuffled to the waist-high rail that divided the courtroom. Murmurs rippled through the crowd—standing against the walls, seated shoulder to shoulder on the hard wooden benches.

All of them watching me.

Me, Daniel Markham. Accused of piracy and villainy upon the high seas.

Before me, the judge's bench towered, a formidable fortress. On the wall behind the bench were the king's arms, and above that the silver oar of the judge of the Admiralty. The judge peered down from his great height, his eyes small and unsympathetic in a pink, fleshy face.

My hands itched to hold my locket, for it had always been a source of comfort and strength. The locket and the treasure map were still on my person, for though I had been searched, an elderly jailer had let me keep the locket, moved by my tears. And though he had made me remove my crossbelt during the search, he had seemed unconcerned when I fastened it around me afterward.

I knew I looked the guilty wretch—hair to my shoulders, matted, crawling with lice, a scruffy beard, my clothes now grayed and tattered as the sails of a neglected ship, barefooted. Likely I stank too. After six months in jail my world was filled with stink.

The judge frowned, his voice thundering through the rafters of Boston's Town House. "Read the indictment against the prisoner."

"That Daniel Markham, on the seventh day of January in the eighth year of the reign of our sovereign lord King William, did, against the peace of God, upon the high and open seas, piratically and feloniously set upon one ship *Mercury*, during which time the captain was slain and the men placed in bodily fear of their lives. . . ."

Dressed in silver-buckled shoes, silk stockings, breeches, pale blue silk coat reaching to his thighs, waistcoat, and powdered wig, the secretary read in a flat monotone, as if he were reading instructions on how to thread a needle.

"He did feloniously and piratically steal, take, and carry away her tackle, apparel and furniture, ninety pieces of weaponry, fifteen tons of bread, two hundred pair of woolen stockings, one hundred barrels of wine and rum, and three hundred ten pounds in gold specie."

A vast numbness crept through my mind, as if he were talking about someone else—someone who had committed terrible, vile acts against humanity. I scarce heard his voice now, droning from across an entire ocean. On and on he read. The *Jedda* . . . the *Surat Merchant* . . .

The list of charges was long. So long . . .

Robbery . . .

Murder . . .

Terror . . .

For months I'd lain in my cell, day after day, hour after hour, awaiting rescue. And as each month passed to the next, I gradually understood that there would be no rescue. The pirates had deserted me. Josiah had deserted me. Surely they had heard of my fate. All of Boston was talking about it, the jailer had told me. If only they could have captured Josiah Black, everyone was saying, a villain if there ever was one. But they had Daniel Markham instead—once such a nice boy, grandson of the former governor, now a bloodthirsty pirate. Daniel Halfhand, they called me.

I only hoped that once I was allowed to speak in my defense, everyone would recognize my innocence. I'd been told that innocence never failed to shine forth, which was why, they said, I did not require an attorney and must perforce make my own defense.

The judge was speaking to me. "How sayest thou, Daniel Markham? Art thou guilty of this piracy and robbery or not guilty?"

"Not guilty." My voice, a whisper.

"Eh? Pray speak up."

"Not guilty."

"How wilt thou be tried?"

I blinked, confused, my knees trembling. What was I to say? "Sir, I—I beg you, I am ignorant of the proceedings."

The judge's face did not soften. There was a titter of laughter from behind me. I saw the frowns from the twelve men seated in the jury box, all merchants and shipowners of Boston. "How wilt thou be tried? You must answer, 'By God and my country.'"

"By God and my country."

"Call for witnesses."

The crier stood. "Hear ye! Hear ye! If anyone can inform my lords the king's justices, the king's sergeant, the king's attorney general, or His Majesty's advocate in his High Court of Admiralty, of the piracy and robbery whereof the prisoner at the bar stands accused, let them come forth, and they shall be heard."

After a moment of silence, rain spattering the windows, there followed a rustling in the audience. The whisper of clothes. Steps upon the planked floor. The tap of a walking stick. Then, to my dismay, five men joined me at the bar. Three I did not recognize, yet two I knew: one of the men who'd been playing cards aboard the *Jedda*, and the captain of the man-o'-war, who had thrown me into the brig. All of them were dressed in fine silks and laces, one crinkling his face at me in disgust, pressing an embroidered handkerchief over his nose.

"This court recognizes one Benjamin Lewis of Boston, mariner and first mate aboard the merchant ship *Mercury*. The rest of you may be seated until called forward."

Mr. Lewis approached the witness stand and was sworn in.

The attorney general, a finely dressed and bewigged gentleman with a face like a bloodhound, strolled before the witness stand. Whenever he glanced at me, it was as if I did not exist, as if I was already guilty, hanged, buried, and forgotten. "Pray, Mr. Lewis, will you give my lords and the jury an account of what you know of the prisoner and his part in the capture of the *Mercury*?"

With a few clearings of the throat and a cough or two, Mr. Lewis began. "We approached the ship—the, uh, *Tempest Galley*—

on account of the man who stood at her masthead. On account that he was waving a flag that appeared to have blood on it. We thought they were in trouble and required our assistance. Perhaps they did not have a doctor aboard."

"But I was only trying to—" I began.

"Silence!" thundered the judge, pinning me with a baleful stare. I shrank back, manacles and leg irons clanking.

People shifted on the hard-backed benches behind me, and I heard whispers, laughter.

The judge hammered his gavel, his periwig flapping like a sail, wig powder dusting his black robes. "I will have order!" With a scowl, he pointed the gavel at me. "One more word from the prisoner and I will have you gagged. Do not speak unless spoken to. You will have an opportunity for your defense after the witnesses have spoken." The judge straightened his wig. "Proceed."

I was the one who had lured them to the ship, Mr. Lewis testified. Aye, he recognized me, for I had spent all day at the masthead, on the lookout for more ships, coming down late at night to fight and kill one of my fellow pirates.

The prosecutor frowned. "He killed one of his fellow cutthroats, you say?"

"Pushed him off the mast, and then came down and kicked him when he was dead, meanwhile shouting murderous oaths. That's when Captain Black—"

"Do not call him a captain. He is a pirate."

"Certainly. My apologies. That's when Josiah Black took him to his cabin. They seemed very familiar with each other. Josiah Black called him 'Daniel, my boy.'"

"And when the *Mercury* was finally released, did the prisoner make any attempt to go aboard her and thus forsake the life of robbery and villainy?"

"No, my lord, he did not."

"Did there appear to be any attempt by the pirates to hold him against his will?"

"No, my lord."

Two more witnesses from the *Mercury* testified likewise. My chest burned with the desire to speak on my behalf, to tell them the truth—that I was a forced man, that I'd done none of this of my own accord, that I'd been trying to warn them. But I dared not utter a word.

And then the man from the *Jedda* testified. I remembered him. I remembered asking him if he spoke English, and his blank look of incomprehension.

But he'd been lying, for now he spoke in perfect King's English. "He burst into the captain's cabin with the rest of his gang of cutthroats. They put pistols to our heads and commanded us to surrender the ship or they would kill us all."

"Pray, go on."

"That man there—the prisoner—told us his name was Daniel Markham, and if we didn't move, we wouldn't be hurt. He then held us and all the passengers prisoner at the bow. He kept smiling."

Again the prosecutor frowned, glancing briefly at me. "Smiling?"

"Yes, as if he enjoyed our plight. He kept smiling and waving his pistols. We were very much afraid. The women and children were crying, believing themselves about to be murdered."

"Did he take his portion of the share?"

"Doubtless he did, for he seemed to be part and parcel of that murderous lot."

"But you do not know that for certain."

"No, sir. Not for certain."

I stared at the floor. At the dust gathered in the corners of the room. At the polished gold buckles on the attorney's shoes as he paced, turned, paced. At his silk stockings, bunched slightly around his bony ankles.

This cannot be happening.

After a few more questions the witness was dismissed, and Captain Wellington of the man-o'-war was called and sworn in. I remembered his pale blue eyes staring at me, his voice that of a man accustomed to instant obedience. He had shown no pity for me then, and I knew he would show none for me now.

"Sewn in the lining of his coat, you say?" the attorney was asking.

"Indeed. Gold, silver, rubies, emeralds, diamonds, pearls. A treasure worthy of a king."

I shifted my feet as the crowd gasped. My face burned, miserably realizing for the thousandth time that I'd set a trap for myself. *Such a fool I was!*

"Pray tell me, good captain, how a man who is, shall we say, *forced* into piracy comes into possession of such treasure."

"Only by devious means."

"No further questions." So saying, the prosecutor then turned to me. "If the prisoner at the bar will ask any questions of any of the witnesses, he may."

Blood rushed to my head until it thundered in my ears like the roar of a cannon. I licked my dry, cracked lips. "Cap-Captain Wellington—"

"Pray, speak up, boy," ordered the judge. "And do not address the captain directly. You will address the court."

"I desire to know whether I turned myself over to Captain Wellington willingly."

The prosecutor turned to the captain. "He desires to know whether he turned himself over to you willingly."

"Yes, he appears to have done so."

"And I desire to know," I continued, "whether that does not speak of my innocence."

Again the prosecutor repeated the question.

Captain Wellington smiled at me as if looking upon an errant child who did not understand. "Perhaps the prisoner intended to collect the reward for the capture of Josiah Black—I do not know. But as to the prisoner's innocence or guilt, that is not for me to decide. I leave that to the esteemed gentlemen of the jury." Captain Wellington exchanged glances with the jury. There were knowing nods and smiles.

"There was a document," I continued, "attesting to my innocence. It was in my coat."

"Ah," said Captain Wellington. "The coat lined with jewels and coins?"

Again a ripple of laughter echoed through the room, and the judge hammered his gavel. Once the courtroom settled, the captain continued. "Yes, there was a paper, indeed. But it was illegible. Messily written, smudged with grease, and water-stained. The jury can see for themselves."

The prosecutor handed a familiar paper to one of the men in the jury box. He squinted, adjusted his spectacles, held it up to the light, then passed it around as more and more men shook their heads and clucked their tongues.

It's useless, I realized. *They cannot read it. Besides, even if they could, it would not matter.*

"Have you anything more to say?" the prosecutor was asking me, looking pleased with himself.

All the months lying in my cell, straw reeking beneath me, with nothing but hard biscuit to eat, scummy water to drink, my single blanket crawling with vermin, I'd thought of all the questions I'd ask the witnesses, of the marvelous words I'd say to prove my innocence. But now all my brilliance seemed naught but foolishness. And I knew.

I am guilty.

Perhaps not of all of it—I was innocent of any wrongdoings concerning the *Mercury*—but I had indeed participated in the capture of both the *Jedda* and the *Surat Merchant*. I had made grenadoes. I had worked as a powder monkey. I had swarmed aboard with the pirates and fought alongside them. I had willingly taken my share. I had, in fact, to my everlasting horror, killed a man. And because of our attack, every man aboard the *Surat Merchant* had perished when she burned and sank. I was a pirate, a thief, and a murderer.

God forgive me, I thought, hanging my head.

The prosecutor stopped pacing the floor. I could feel him looking at me. "Have you any witnesses to call forward who can attest to your supposed innocence?"

"No, my lord," I whispered.

"Well, then, may it please your lordship—"

There was a rustle behind me and the squeak of a wooden bench. Then someone spoke. "If—if it please the court, kind sirs, I—I will speak on his behalf."

That voice—I recognize it.

I raised my head. A ray of hope sparked within me.

It was Faith!

CHAPTER
25

*F*aith was thinner than I remembered. Her clothing plain, patched. Skin pale and pasty. Brown hair pulled back tightly. White cap upon her head, tied beneath her chin.

She wept easily while standing at the bar, her eyes red and watery, her voice trembling. She told them about the capture of the *Gray Pearl,* about my protecting her, about the murder of Robert Markham, about our capture by pirates. She told them about her illness, of my coming to see her, of her being released to a doctor's care at Newport, Rhode Island.

"Pray tell the court, Mistress Markham," said the prosecutor, "why the prisoner did not also stay behind at Newport when he had the opportunity."

Faith glanced at me, lips trembling.

"He—he told me that the pirates were holding him hostage. That if I talked, if I said anything to anyone about what I'd seen, they would—they would *kill* him."

"I see. Isn't it possible, Mistress Markham, that the prisoner willingly chose the life of robbery and plunder upon the high seas and merely told you a lie?"

"Why, no. Daniel had no reason to lie."

"Embarking upon a life of robbery and plunder is no reason to lie?"

Faith blinked, as if not understanding.

The prosecutor paced before the witness stand, continuing. "If it was not a lie, then surely someone else must have also told you that Daniel Markham was a hostage, held against his will? The pirate Josiah Black, perhaps?"

I heard Faith swallow, so still was the courtroom. "Please understand, I—I was very ill. It is possible that someone said something, but I was too ill to recollect—"

Frowning, the prosecutor stopped pacing and stared at Faith. "Mistress Markham, I am a bit confused. Please help me understand. According to your *recollection,* the prisoner, accused of treachery upon the high seas, told you he was a hostage. Is this correct?"

"Yes."

"Yet you say you cannot recall if anyone else spoke to you regarding the matter, because you were too ill at the time. Is this also correct?"

Faith lowered her head, not answering, tears slipping down her cheeks.

"How can they both be true, Mistress Markham? Were you in right possession of your faculties, or were you not?"

She sniffed into her handkerchief. "My lord, I *was* in right possession of my faculties. I remember—" Suddenly she clamped her mouth shut, her face stricken.

"Yes?" the prosecutor prompted.

"Nothing. It was nothing."

"May I remind you, Mistress Markham, that you are under oath. Pray tell the court exactly what you remember. To do otherwise is a sin against God."

Every drop of blood seemed to drain from Faith's countenance. She twisted her handkerchief. Tears slid off her chin. When she finally spoke, her voice was a whisper. "J-Josiah Black spoke to me briefly before I was taken ashore at Newport."

"Yes?"

"He said—he said it was best that I not say anything about what I had seen, as he could not vouch for the gentlemanly conduct of his men."

"I see. And what else did this Josiah Black say?"

Faith looked at me, her face crumpling, a picture of misery. "I'm sorry, Daniel. Oh please believe me—I'm so sorry."

"Answer the question."

Between tiny, hiccuping sobs, she answered. "Josiah Black said—he said to get well and to not worry, for he would take care of Daniel and be certain he came to no harm."

There was a collective gasp in the courtroom, a cry of "No further questions!" from the prosecutor, the pounding of the gavel, after which followed a few moments in which the only sound was that of Faith weeping.

Then the prosecutor addressed me. "Have you any questions for the witness?"

I was deeply moved by Faith's willingness to stand before the court, to testify on my behalf. Tears clouded my eyes. I scarce found my voice. "I desire the court to thank Mistress Markham for what she has done and for what she has tried to do. She is a brave and worthy woman."

The prosecutor raised his eyebrows but relayed my message nonetheless.

After that, everything happened swiftly.

The prosecutor made his closing remarks. Thunderous. Impressive. Words lofty and pretentious as the judge's bench.

I was escorted to a small holding cell while the jury deliberated.

I was brought back and again placed before the bar.

A deathly hush pressed upon the courtroom.

"Gentlemen of the jury," said the judge, "are you all agreed of your verdict?"

"Yes."

"Who shall say for you?"

"Our foreman."

"Hold up thy hand. Look upon the prisoner. Is Daniel Markham guilty of the piracy and robbery whereof he stands accused, or not guilty?"

"Guilty."

The judge turned his small eyes to me. "Daniel Markham, you stand convicted. The law for the heinousness of your crime hath appointed a severe punishment, by an ignominious death, and the judgment which the law awards is this: that you shall be taken from hence to the place from whence you came, and from thence to the place of execution, and that there you shall be hanged by the neck until you be dead. And the Lord have mercy upon you."

On a misty November morning, the day appointed for me to die, I was taken from the Boston jailhouse.

The provost marshal led the procession. He carried the silver oar—the emblem of his authority over the Admiralty Court. Behind him marched his officers, then the town constables, a minister, then me, flanked by forty musketeers.

My breath plumed white. The cold of the cobblestones stung my bare feet.

Onlookers jammed Great Street. They jeered and laughed, cried, prayed, exhorted, and sang hymns. Fathers held children on their shoulders for a better view of me. Someone threw a soft tomato, which hit one of the musketeers on the arm and splattered my face. Another threw a rotten egg, the stink of sulfur making my stomach roil, bringing back memories of a battle that now seemed so long ago.

Today I will die. . . .

The minister had his Bible open, his mouth moving. "The Lord watches over all who love him, but all the wicked he will destroy. . . ."

"Pray for forgiveness, child," said one woman as I passed.

"A longer neck will suit thee well!" hollered a man, grinning.

"Go back to hell where you belong, you eight-fingered spawn of the devil!"

"You have shamed the memory of your grandfather!"

"Mercy, Lord, mercy on his soul!"

Today I will die. . . .

"Daniel!"

It was Faith. She hurried alongside the procession, panting, pushing people aside. A child bounced in her arms.

"Faith!" My voice cracked.

She was crying. Her babe was crying, mucus dribbling into his mouth. "Fear not! The good Lord loves you!"

Then I was crying too, eyes stinging, choking out my words. "I'm sorry for anything I've ever done that has hurt you. Pray forgive me!"

"Daniel, the good Lord loves you! You are always forgiven! Always! Do not be afraid!"

"Blasphemer!" shouted the minister, his face twisting. "The Holy Scriptures tell us, 'On the wicked he will rain coals of fire and sulfur; a scorching wind shall be the portion of their cup'!"

Faith stumbled and fell behind, her cap now dangling from the tie about her throat. Strands of hair stuck to her sodden cheeks. The child sucked a finger and stared at me, sniffling.

"Is he my brother?"

"Aye. His name's little Robert. He looks like his father."

A musketeer prodded me in the ribs with the butt of his musket. "Move along, Halfhand."

"Bless you!" cried Faith. "Bless you!" Falling to her knees, she burst into a freshet of tears.

At Scarlett's Wharf they shoved me into a boat. I stumbled against the hull, lying there until they yanked me upright. My mouth was cut, and I felt a trickle of blood. I almost asked the constable to loosen my bindings, as my wrists ached and my hands throbbed, but then realized that in just a few moments it would not matter. Nothing would matter.

Today I will die. . . .

A great grief pushed against my breastbone, raw, making it hard to breathe.

It should not have been this way.

We pulled away from shore. Now all was silent except for the creak of the oarlocks and the soft dip of the oars. A lone gull soared overhead.

In the mouth of the Charles River, between the ebb and flow of the tide, foundation mired deep into the mud below the water's surface, a scaffold thrust out of the low-lying mist like a skeleton. Raw bones of wood, stark against the leaden sky. We bumped against the scaffold platform, a hollow thunk of wood on wood. One of the men stepped onto the floating platform and tied the boat's line. Then they forced me to my feet and onto the platform. The scaffold creaked, groaned.

My legs were like jelly.

They turned me to face the crowd.

Men jammed the railings of the many ships. They straddled the yards and hung from the shrouds, some climbing higher for a better look. Hundreds, maybe thousands of people lined the shore. Crammed shoulder to shoulder upon Scarlett's Wharf. Crowded upon Broughton's Hill. Hundreds more surrounded the scaffold, huddled in small boats, cloaks wrapped tight against the cold, the lower halves of their bodies lost in the mist, as if they were corpses rising from a watery grave.

Hungry. All of them. Hungry to see me hanged . . .

The minister stood in the boat, legs braced wide, holding his Bible open. Into the silence he proceeded to give a sermon on the justice of God. The punishment for those who committed crimes against humanity. The lake of fire and brimstone that most assuredly awaited me. The suffering of eternal torment . . . His words became a blur, one long word drawn out forever.

"I said, have you any last words?" someone was asking me.

I stared at him, blinking, as if trying to comprehend who he was. Why I was here.

And then the hangman was placing the noose around my neck, the hemp rough, scratchy. He positioned the knot against the back of my head and tightened the noose.

Dear God, it has come to this. . . .

They left the scaffold then and climbed back into the boat, everyone seated once again on the thwarts, watching me. Someone gave a signal and the platform beneath my feet began to sink.

Dear God, have mercy. . . .

At that moment, a man in one of the nearby boats stood,

threw off his cloak, and drew his pistols, aiming one at the provost marshal and the other at the minister.

"Stop the execution," he said.

It was Josiah Black.

I was struggling already.

Standing on tiptoe.

The platform still sinking. Slowly.

The noose about my neck tightening.

"Help!" I gasped.

"Release him!" commanded Josiah, cocking both pistols.

The provost marshal had gone pale. The minister said nothing, eyes wide.

"'Tis Josiah Black!" cried the provost marshal.

"I offer my life in exchange for his! Decide now or I will blow you to hell!"

The tips of my toes scraping the planks. The rope, so tight. My head pounding with blood. The world turning black.

The platform, sinking, sinking, sinking.

"Set the prisoner free and arrest Josiah Black for piracy and murder! We have him, men, we finally have him!"

"Upon your honor as gentlemen?"

"Aye, upon our honor . . ."

CHAPTER
26

They gave us five minutes only.

Five minutes.

Josiah gripped the iron bars, his eyes black in the feeble light. "You came," he said.

"They would not let me come before," I replied, my voice a whisper, my throat swollen.

And then we stood, awkwardly.

"Does your neck pain you?" he asked finally.

I touched my neck. After four days it was still sore, bruised, an ugly purple welt stretching under my jaw from one ear to the other. I nodded, remembering, still hardly able to believe that I was the one now free and he the one condemned to die.

The very day he had offered his life in exchange for mine, they had taken Josiah to the Town House, where he'd pled guilty. Scarce had he finished uttering the word than they sentenced him to death—gleefully, almost, hardly able to keep the smiles from their faces. They had furthermore condemned his body to hang in irons at Bird Island for two years—a warning to all mariners lest their feet take a fancy to villainy.

"Do you have need of anything?" Josiah asked. His voice, so silken, so . . . so . . . *kind*.

"I—I don't know. I don't think so."

"Do you have a place to stay?"

"At my father's house. Faith has been living there this past year. Her son's name is Robert."

"Robert. That's a good name."

"Aye."

Josiah paused, then took the bottom corner of his jacket in hand. Breaking a thread in the seam, tugging it apart, he reached inside the lining and pulled out a woman's ring, a pearl surrounded by tiny diamonds. "It was your mother's," he said, handing it to me through the bars. "It was all I had of her. Besides you, of course."

He dropped the ring onto my palm. I could say nothing, my throat tight. Hurting.

"Daniel—"

"Aye."

"You were always a good boy. Pray forgive me for the things I have done."

At the end of the hall, a key rattled in the lock, echoing. Then they were approaching. The constable, keys jangling in his hands. Six musketeers, boots tramping, faces hard.

It was then I became aware of the sounds outside. Dogs barking, the excited yell of the crowd, shouting, laughter, prayers.

It was time.

And all the things I had wanted to say, still unsaid.

I closed my hand over the ring. Josiah was still looking at me. My throat filled; my eyes stung. I stood there looking back at him, feeling something inside me burst open, as if it could stay hidden no longer. "I always loved you," I said, lips trembling.

"I know, Daniel, my boy. Do not let it trouble you now. Be at peace."

The constable pushed me aside, placing a key in the lock of Josiah's cell. "Your time is finished," he was saying. "You will proceed from hence to the place of execution."

I was crying now. And as the door to the jail cell opened, I rushed inside, hearing the curses from the guards, and threw myself into my father's arms. Hands grabbed me from behind, but Josiah wrapped his arms tightly around me.

"Father!" I cried. "Don't die! Don't do this. Why did you have to come back?"

"Daniel, Daniel," he said softly. "It was the only way."

"No, Father, no!"

They wrenched me from his grasp.

"Father!"

They marched him away, down the hall.

Josiah was turning back, saying, "Go fetch what you left behind in Madagascar, Daniel. Live a life of goodness! A life of charity and mercy! Do what I could not!"

And then they were outside, where the provost marshal was waiting with his silver oar, where the minister waited with his Bible, where the crowd waited with their soft tomatoes and rotten eggs.

EPILOGUE

*O*n the sixth day of November in the year of our Lord 1698, they hanged Josiah Black for piracy and murder.

I pushed my way through the crowds until I stood atop Broughton's Hill. And there, from a distance, I watched my father pass from this world into the next. I watched because I could not bear to leave him to suffer and die alone.

Late that night, not long after the town crier had announced, "One o'clock and all's well!" I rowed out to the scaffold and took my father's body down. For a long time I wept, holding him in my arms on the scaffold, forgiving him of every wrong he had ever committed, crying until I had no more tears left, until my legs stiffened and my head throbbed.

Then, with a strength beyond me, I pulled him into the boat and rowed ashore.

With the assistance of a shovel, a small cart, and a sheet of canvas, I conveyed my father's body to the churchyard. And there, beside my mother, I buried him.

An unmarked grave.

I have visited it many years since, and so it remains. . . .

There is a peace that abides with me now. A peace of understanding, knowing the failings and weaknesses of my parents—my mother and both my fathers—but loving them nonetheless. And I have learned that there is enough love for all of them, and to spare.

Sometimes I feel as if they are watching me. As if they see me as I go about this life here, and they approve and are themselves happy.

I believe that life is good. That life is filled with sweetness and honor and charity if one seeks it, if one does not look elsewhere.

It is a gift my parents have given me.

It is a gift Faith has given me.

And for that, I give thanks.

If you happen to peek in the windows of Boston's orphanage, you might find it passing strange that the children are warmly dressed, clad in fine clothes from head to foot, with new primers, new slates, a new stove or two, ample wood for the winter, and plenty to eat. You also might find it strange that the gravedigger of the churchyard now lives in a grand house, and that the grave of Abigail

Ball Markham and the adjacent plot of grass are so well cared for, adorned with fresh flowers whenever they are in season. Let us not forget Timothy's mother, the Widow Allsworth, who for all intents and purposes should have been in the poorhouse, but who instead has ten new dresses every year, an abundance of food, a five-year supply of candles in her storeroom, and her taxes paid to the very last penny.

The key to such strange occurrences is found upon Jamaica's northern shore, where the breezes are warm and the sands soft and sugary, where there lies a sizeable plantation. If you care to listen closely, you will hear laughter. A young boy plays with the island children, his schoolmates. They chase one another beneath the coconut palms and lie under the shade of the banana trees when the sun becomes too warm. You might not recognize the boy's mother, but perhaps you would. She is rosy-cheeked, her eyes vibrant, and there is a skip to her step each morning as she walks to the new schoolhouse to teach the local children their letters. And when she returns home, she is greeted by a young man, Daniel Black by name, sun-browned and strong, one who loves her as a brother loves a sister. And who is to say what the years hold in store? But that is beyond our tale. For now, for this moment, it is enough.

AUTHOR'S
NOTE

Pirates have always captured our imaginations. They swashbuckled under the Jolly Roger, kidnapped beautiful princesses, and danced merry jigs. Treasure chests bursting with diamonds, emeralds, and gold were buried on palm-studded islands. Peg legs, eye patches, parrots—these images have been perpetuated through movies and books. We love our pirates. Their easy lifestyle appeals to us. They are a symbol of freedom, answering to no one but themselves. But with so much fiction that glamorizes piracy—emphasizing the gallant and downplaying the atrocious—it is easy to forget the barbarities that were often perpetrated by pirates. David Cordingly, a respected authority on pirates, says, ". . . it is important to keep in mind who these people really were—all of them thieves, and some of them murderers. Some of their acts were so barbarous—mutilating people, torturing their victims—that their eventual decline must be viewed with relief."[1]

Piracy was nothing more than grand theft at sea. We see nothing glamorous about muggers nowadays, who shove a gun in your face and demand your wallet, or robbers who hold up the corner mini-mart. Pirates throughout history terrorized their victims. They chased down merchant vessels and swarmed aboard, swinging their cutlasses and brandishing their pistols, using terror as a weapon to induce submission. In most cases, if the horrified victims cooperated, no harm was done except for the inevitable looting. But if there was resistance, by the time the pirates finished, often the deck was strewn with dead bodies or the ship itself was ablaze. The world quickly learned to offer no resistance.

So then, is all pirate fiction merely that—fiction? Not at all. Because of the violence of their occupation, pirates indeed lost limbs and eyes. Preferring warmer climes, they frequented tropical islands, where some did adopt parrots for pets. And it is a documented fact that pirates captured treasures of jewels and gold while Jolly Rogers or bloody flags flew atop their mainmasts (although they were more likely to capture a "treasure" of socks, molasses, and flour). And, like any group of individuals, pirates varied from those who conducted themselves with panache and chivalry, to the vast majority who were foulmouthed, hard-drinking, quick to violence, and finally to those who would likely be our serial killers of today. Yet the atrocities have been forgotten, while the dashing romance has thrived, captivating the hearts of audiences, especially children's, for centuries. This has caused us to view pirates through a surreal lens, glimpsing only caricatures of the actual men.

With *Voyage of Plunder*, I sought to help readers experience the real-life drama and terror that went hand in hand with piracy. What would it really be like to be boarded by pirates? I also fashioned the pirates in *Voyage of Plunder* after actual pirates. Gideon Fist was patterned after Blackbeard, a pirate who lived during the Golden Age of Piracy (approximately 1691–1723), a terrifying giant of a man who went into battle with lighted matches stuck beneath his hat so that the smoke swirled about his enormous beard, making it appear to be on fire.[2] Josiah Black was modeled after two infamous pirates: Thomas Tew and Henry Every, who were active in the late 1600s, when men made "the Round" to the Red Sea.

Piracy began flourishing in the American colonies when England passed the first of the Navigation Acts in 1651, forcing colonists to trade exclusively with British ships. Goods imported into the colonies were now priced exorbitantly, while exported goods were sold for a song. Desperate to help themselves, many of the colonists turned to smuggling and piracy. Some high-ranking officials financed pirates and their vessels, taking a cut of the booty upon the pirates' return. Pirated goods flooded the colonies. Pirates were given hospitality and protection. One governor even married his daughter to a pirate to help establish the pirate in a new political career! Often pirates were given fake privateering commissions. Privateers were granted permission by their respective governments to attack and plunder the ships of enemy nations—a time-honored and acceptable method of war. The confiscated goods belonged to the government, less a percentage for the privateering captain and crew. A fake commission was used as a cover for good old-fashioned piracy.

In 1692, Thomas Tew received a commission from the governor to attack a French outpost on the Guinea coast. But once at sea, Tew had other ideas. Captain Charles Johnson, author of the definitive and seminal book *A General History of the Robberies and Murders of the Most Notorious Pyrates,* published in 1724, wrote: "[Tew proposed] to shape a Course which should lead them to Ease and Plenty, in which they might pass the rest of their Days. That one bold Push would do their Business, and they might return home, not only without Danger, but even with Reputation. The Crew finding he expected their Resolution, cry'd out, one and all, 'A gold Chain, or a wooden Leg, we'll stand by you,' "[3] a statement echoed by the crews of the *Tempest Galley,* the *Defiance,* and the *Sweet Jamaica.*

Tew and his ship, the *Amity,* entered the Red Sea, and in July 1693 fell upon the Mogul's flagship of the treasure fleet. When the *Amity* received no resistance, Tew and his men gathered up a treasure worth in excess of £100,000 (about $62 million today) in gems, silks, bars of gold, spices, and "elephants' teeth."[4]

Arriving fresh from his exploits at Newport, Rhode Island, Tew became an instant sensation and was entertained by such respected men of society as the governor of New York. Merchants from Boston, like Robert Markham, swooped down to Newport to snatch up the booty. News of the coup reached the ears of every young man—sons of rich planters, of poor farmers, of struggling merchants—and by the time Tew was outfitted for another voyage, they all clamored to be a part of his crew. Piracy reached a fever pitch, and ships by the tens and hundreds left the colonies to seek their fortunes upon the high seas.[5]

Henry Every, known as the "grand pirate," needed no such encouragement. Already second mate aboard a privateer, Every took control of the vessel, ousting the captain and a few loyal men. "You must know," Every told the captain, "that I am Captain of this Ship now, and this is my Cabin, therefore you must walk out; I am bound to Madagascar, with a Design of making my own Fortune, and that of all the brave Fellows joined with me."[6] Every then sailed to Madagascar, where a number of pirates and their ships joined forces with him.

In August 1695, Every, in command of his formidable fleet, arrived at the mouth of the Red Sea. One of the sloops was the *Amity*, captained by Thomas Tew. The first ship they attacked was the *Fateh Muhammed*, one of the ships of the Mogul of India's grand treasure fleet. Although they captured £50,000 in gold and silver, Tew was downed by a shot to his belly, dying as did Timothy in *Voyage of Plunder*, "who held his Bowels with his Hands some small Space. . . ."[7]

Despite Tew's death, Every next set his sights on the *Ganj-I-Sawai* (which means "Exceeding Treasure"). This formidable vessel was carrying 400 soldiers, 80 cannon, and a number of passengers on pilgrimage to Mecca.[8] Although she was the largest ship in the Mogul's fleet, Every succeeded in overwhelming her in a two-hour battle. The booty from this victory was so great, each pirate's portion came to £1,000. This was a staggering amount of money, as an average sailor earned only £1.66 in one month's honest work. It is estimated that the loot from both catches totaled as much as £325,000, or the equivalent of $200 million today![9] The captures made in *Voyage of Plunder* are loosely modeled after Tew's earlier seizure of the Mogul's flagship and Every's overpowering of the *Ganj-I-Sawai*.

Eventually, piracy in the Atlantic Ocean and the Red Sea became so out of control, so embarrassing, wresting so-called "fair trade" out of England's hands and outraging the Indian government, that England responded by tightening the noose on piracy in the colonies. The governor of New York was replaced as were other pirate supporters, and there was a bounty placed on many of the pirates, including Every. Robert Markham and Josiah Black would have been swept up in this zeal to strangle piracy. Pirates were no longer welcomed into the community with open arms, but were now captured, tried, and hanged as criminals. One pirate who came to such an unhappy end was Captain William Kidd, a man commissioned to sail to the Red Sea to hunt down pirates, but who supposedly turned pirate himself. Following a web of political intrigue, including the convenient "loss" of key documents, Kidd, former pewholder and respected member of New York society, was tried for piracy. In 1701, he was hanged, his body tarred and wrapped in iron bands and his remains suspended from a gibbet at Thames's Tilbury Point for several years afterward.[10] Kidd's infamous ship, the *Adventure Galley*, a sleek, fast warship, was the prototype for Josiah Black's ship, the *Tempest Galley*.

In all likelihood, had Daniel been captured and accused of piracy as he was in 1698, he would have been taken to the Admiralty Courts in London for trial. But for the sake of simplicity, and because only two years later England granted authority to the colonies to try, condemn, and execute pirates,[11] I brought Daniel to Boston. Pirates tried in Boston were indeed hanged on gallows that were located in the mouth of the Charles River, accessible only by boat; if they were particularly notorious, their remains hung at Bird Island. Much of the dialogue in Daniel's trial is taken from actual trial transcripts, including the trial of 1696 in which six men from Henry Every's crew were found guilty and executed.

A desire for riches wasn't the only motivating factor in becoming a pirate. Life on a merchant vessel was hard; the food was meager and unappetizing, the work demanding and dangerous, mortality rates high, and the pay low. Dr. Samuel Johnson says, "No man will be a sailor who has contrivance enough to get himself into a jail; for being in a ship is being in a jail, with the chance of being drowned. . . . A man in a jail has more room, better food, and commonly better company."[12] And then, of course, merchant or naval seamen had to deal with discipline meted out by the captain in a day when it was believed that physical punishment kept men in line. In *Voyage of Plunder,* Timothy recounts how "Captain Hewitt hung a basket of grapeshot around some poor fellow's neck and tied his arms to the capstan bars until blood burst from his nose and mouth. The basket must've weighed two hundred pounds or more"—an incident based upon a true event.[13] This case and many like it, to be sure, are extreme. History is only aware of them because these incidents were reported and brought before the courts. The captains who treated their crews fairly and with appropriate discipline did not come under the court's scrutiny and of them history remains unaware. But the basic concept itself, that men would only obey if made to fear authority, was prone to corruption at its core and could not help but foster such atrocities.

Small wonder, then, when such a ship was captured by pirates, that the allure of the "easy life" would have sparkled like diamonds for many of the merchant crew. Other men became pirates when international wars ended, glutting the harbor towns with out-of-work sailors. Others crossed the fine line between privateering and piracy. And still others abandoned their life of poverty on land—where jobs were scarce and wages abysmal, where the laws allowed a person to be hanged for shoplifting or pickpocketing—[14] taking to the life of piracy, where men treated one another with equality and where no one was in authority over another.

The pirate democracy was the first democracy of its kind for the workingman, in which officers were elected, issues were decided by consensus, and all provisions and prizes shared in common. What a difference this must have made to the average fellow who lived in a time of demanded obeisance to governing authorities and who had no voice regarding laws, wages, taxes, and wars. The Articles in *Voyage of Plunder* were taken from the actual Articles of Bartholomew Roberts, alias Black Bart, a great pirate captain killed in battle in 1722.[15] Most pirate ships had similar Articles, providing liberty and equality to all—black and white—including a form of social security in the event of disability.

During the height of piracy in the Red Sea, Madagascar became a safe haven for pirates, most particularly the island of St. Mary's. The St. Mary's depicted in *Voyage of Plunder* is as accurate as history allows, including Adam Baldridge, who had built fortifications complete with cannon, and who acted as supplier to pirates. (Other than King William, Adam Baldridge is the only character in *Voyage of Plunder* that is not fictional.) The integrated and egalitarian society the pirates experienced with the Malagasy was remarkable during a time of imperialistic colonization, when native peoples were treated as non-equals, or worse, as slaves. The pleasant harmony established on St. Mary's was disrupted, however, when Baldridge sold some of the natives into slavery. Naturally outraged, the Malagasy rose in rebellion. Baldridge escaped, and relations between the pirates and the Malagasy were soon mended; life went on on St. Mary's as before.[16]

Despite the atrocities committed, there is, indeed, much to

be admired about pirates. These colorful characters, defying the role society had set for them, defined their own sense of place and standard of equality, and we can take comfort in knowing that they will continue to capture our hearts through books and movies that thrill us and set our romantic imaginations ablaze. Yet, as we dream about glittering treasure chests, prattling parrots, razor-sharp cutlasses, and leering black flags, we must remember that their allure depended upon whose ship you were on—the pirates' or the victims'.

1. Cordingly, David, *Under the Black Flag: The Romance and the Reality of Life Among the Pirates* (New York: Random House, Inc., 1995).

2. Johnson, Captain Charles, *A General History of the Robberies and Murders of the Most Notorious Pyrates* (London, 1724), edited by Manuel Schonhorn, author given as Daniel Defoe (Columbia: University of South Carolina Press, 1972), pp. 84–85.

3. Ibid., p. 422.

4. Cordingly, David, ed., *Pirates: Terror on the High Seas—From the Caribbean to the South China Sea* (Atlanta: Turner Publishing, Inc., 1996), p. 147.

5. Botting, Douglas, and the Editors of Time-Life Books, *The Pirates* (Alexandria, Va.: Time-Life Books, 1978).

6. Johnson, Captain Charles, *A General History of the Robberies and Murders of the Most Notorious Pyrates*, p. 51.

7. Ibid., p. 439.

8. Cordingly, David, ed., *Pirates: Terror on the High Seas—From the Caribbean to the South China Sea*, p. 150.

9. Rogoziński, Jan, *Honor Among Thieves: Captain Kidd, Henry Every, and the Pirate Democracy in the Indian Ocean* (Mechanicsburg, Penn.: Stackpole Books, 2000), pp. 87–88.

10. Cordingly, David, ed., *Pirates: Terror on the High Seas—From the Caribbean to the South China Sea*, pp. 158–160.

11. Dow, George Francis, *Every Day Life in the Massachusetts Bay Colony* (New York: Arno Press, 1977).

12. Cordingly, David, ed., *Pirates: Terror on the High Seas—From the Caribbean to the South China Sea*, pp. 128–129.

13. Rediker, Marcus, *Between the Devil and the Deep Blue Sea: Merchant Seamen, Pirates and the Anglo-American Maritime World, 1700–1750* (New York: Cambridge University Press, 1987), pp. 218–219.

14. Sydney, William Connor, *England and the English in the Eighteenth Century*, vols. I & II (Edinburgh: John Grant, 1891), pp. 267–269.

15. Cordingly, David, *Under the Black Flag: The Romance and the Reality of Life Among the Pirates*, pp. 99–100.

16. Rogoziński, Jan, *Honor Among Thieves: Captain Kidd, Henry Every, and the Pirate Democracy in the Indian Ocean*, pp. 56–62.

GLOSSARY
of
SEA TERMS

abaft—toward the stern of a vessel. The word *abaft* is always used in relation to another object—for example, "abaft the mainmast" or "abaft the beam."

abeam—at right angles to the length of a vessel, but not in the vessel itself.

aft—toward the stern of a vessel. An abbreviation of *abaft*.

aloft—above the deck of the ship.

amidships—in the center of the ship.

back-staff—a long, triangular-shaped instrument, used for calculating a ship's position.

backstay—a rope support for the mast, extending from the masthead down to the chains at a ship's side.

ballast—weight added to the bottom of a ship, necessary in balancing the ship upon the waters.

banyan—a fancy nightdress for men, originally worn by Hindu tradesmen.

bilge—an enclosed section at the bottom of the ship where seawater collects.

block—a rounded wooden case that houses a pulley, used

for lowering and lifting heavy loads. A line through a block forms a tackle.

bow—the front of a ship (rhymes with "cow").

bow chaser—a gun in the bow, fired when chasing another vessel.

bowsprit—large wooden pole extending off the bow.

brace—two of a kind, as in "a brace of pistols."

braces—the ropes that work the yards of a vessel.

bulkhead—a wall-like structure in a ship. It separates a vessel into cabins and compartments.

bulwarks—the built-up side walls above the deck of a ship.

cable length—a maritime measure equaling 608 feet.

capstan—barrel-like mechanism, designed for hauling in heavy loads such as an anchor. The capstan is rotated circularly by pushing the long handles that extend like spokes out of the top of the capstan.

careen—to lay a ship on its side for repairs, caulking, and cleaning.

close-hauled—sailing as close to the wind as the ship will allow without the sails luffing.

companionway—a ship's stairway or ladder leading from one deck to another.

courses—the lowest square sails on each mast. They are designated by the name of the mast upon which they're set—for example, "fore course," "main course," and "mizzen course."

crosstrees—pieces of oak set in a horizontal crisscross, located on the upper mast.

cuddy—a small room or cupboard in a ship or boat.

drub—to beat severely.

East Indiaman—a large merchant vessel, belonging to the East India Company, that transported merchandise between Europe and the East Indies. East Indiamen were usually heavily armed, filled with 200 sailors, and avoided by pirates who sought easier prey.

fo'c'sle—the forward area of

a ship, directly behind the bow and in front of the foremast. In the *Tempest Galley,* the area under the fo'c'sle deck was open, but in later ships it was enclosed to provide the crew with sleeping quarters. (*Fo'c'sle* is short for *forecastle* and is pronounced FOKE-sul.)

footrope—the horizontal rope suspended under a yard, upon which sailors stand while reefing or furling the sails.

fore, forward—toward the bow of a ship. The foremast would be the mast closest to the bow.

furl—to roll a sail to a yard.

galloon—a narrow trim of lace, metallic braid, or embroidery, with scalloped edges.

gibbet—a vertical post with a projecting arm from which to hang executed criminals for viewing.

grapeshot—small iron balls shot in a cluster from a cannon.

gunwale—the upper edge of the ship's side (pronounced GUN-ul).

halyard—a rope or line used to hoist sails, yards, flags, etc.

head to wind—to steer a vessel such that its bow (head) faces directly into the wind. Forward momentum is slowed, and if the vessel stays in this position, it comes to a dead stop.

heave to—to trim a vessel's sails aback so that it no longer makes headway.

heel—to lean to one side, especially due to wind action on a ship.

helm—the steering apparatus of a vessel.

hove to—past tense of *heave to.*

hull—the main body of a vessel.

knot—a measure of speed equal to one nautical mile per hour. One nautical mile equals 1.1508 land miles.

leeward—the side of the ship away from the direction of the wind (opposite of *windward;* pronounced LOO-urd).

log—a written record of a ship's voyage recorded by the captain.

luff—to turn a ship close to the wind so that the sails shake and momentum is slowed.

main—the principal or most important part in a three-masted vessel; thus, the center mast is called the *mainmast,* the center hatch the *main hatch,* and so on.

Malagasy—a native of Madagascar.

man-o'-war—a warship.

marlinspike—an iron tool about sixteen inches long, broad at one end and tapering to a point, used to separate strands of rope.

masthead—the top of a mast.

miniature—a small portrait.

mizzen—the third mast, or aftermast, on a three-masted vessel (short for *mizzenmast*).

monsoon—the seasonal winds of southern Asia and the Indian Ocean, blowing from the northeast in winter and from the southwest in summer.

painter—a rope attached to the bow of a boat, used for securing the boat to docks, other vessels, landing places, steps, etc.

pawl—an iron stop used to keep the capstan from unwinding.

periwig—a wig for men, characterized by long, voluminous curls.

pinnace—a small boat propelled by sails or oars.

poop deck—a raised deck at the stern of a ship.

port—the left side of a vessel when facing forward.

quarter—the sides of a ship aft of the ship's waist. *Quarter* is also a term meaning "mercy." "No quarter" meant that there would be no mercy.

quarterdeck—the deck abaft the mainmast.

queue—a braid of hair tied at the back of the head.

ratline—one of the horizontal ropes attached to the shrouds to form a rope ladder (pronounced RAT-lin).

reef—to reduce the amount of sail in operation.

salt horse—salted, dried beef.

scabbard—a sheath for a sword or cutlass.

scimitar—a cutlass with a

deep curve, primarily used by Arabs and Turks.

scuppers—openings cut in the bulwarks to drain seawater.

sheets—lines connected to the lower corners of the sails, used to control the sails.

ship in stays—a ship that has turned head to wind, losing all momentum.

shrapnel—shards of debris flung outward after an explosion or impact.

shroud—a rope, usually one of a pair, that stretches from the top of the mast (the masthead) to the sides of a vessel to support the mast. Sailors climbed the shrouds if they needed to go aloft. The shrouds had horizontal rope rungs called *ratlines*.

snuff—pulverized tobacco, inhaled through the nose or placed between the lip and gums.

specie—money in coin.

starboard—the right side of a vessel when facing forward.

stern—the back of a ship.

stuns'ls—smaller, triangular sails set between the square sails. Intended to maximize wind power and used only in moderate weather and light winds. (*Stuns'ls* is short for *studding sails* and is pronounced STUN-sulz.)

sweeps—very large oars.

tackle—an arrangement of blocks fitted with ropes, used to lift heavy loads.

tar—an informal term for a sailor. *Tar* is a clipped form of *Jack Tar*. It derived from the tendency of sailors to treat their clothing, hats, and even their hair with tar as protection against the weather.

thwarts—the wooden seats in a boat that also provide structural support to the hull.

transom—the flat-ended structure at the very stern of the ship.

waist—the center area of a vessel.

windward—the direction facing the wind (opposite of *leeward*).

yard—a horizontal beam attached to a mast to support a sail.

BIBLIOGRAPHY

Amery, Heather, and G.P.B. Naish. *The Age of Sailing Ships*. London: Usborne Publishing, Ltd., 1976.

Arnold-Forster, F. D. *The Madagascar Pirates*. New York: Lothrop, Lee and Shepard Co., Inc., 1957.

Biddulph, John. *The Pirates of Malabar, and an English Woman in India Two Hundred Years Ago*. London: Smith, Elder & Co., 1907.

Botting, Douglas, and the Editors of Time-Life Books. *The Pirates*. Alexandria, Va.: Time-Life Books, 1978.

Burgess, Robert F., and Carl J. Clausen. *Gold, Galleons and Archaeology*. Indianapolis and New York: Bobbs-Merrill Co., Inc., 1976.

Chidsey, Donald Barr. *The American Privateers*. New York: Dodd, Mead & Co., 1962.

Cochran, Hamilton. *Freebooters of the Red Sea: Pirates, Politicians and Pieces of Eight*. New York: Bobbs-Merrill Co., Inc., 1965.

A Complete Collection of State-Trials and Proceedings upon High-Treason, and Other Crimes and Misdemeanors; from the Reign of King Richard II to the End of the Reign of King George I. 2nd ed., 6 vols. London: Walthoe, 1730.

Copeland, Peter F. *Working Dress in Colonial and Revolutionary America.* Westport, Conn.: Greenwood Press, 1977.

Cordingly, David, ed. *Pirates: Terror on the High Seas—From the Caribbean to the South China Sea.* Atlanta: Turner Publishing, Inc., 1996.

———. *Under the Black Flag: The Romance and the Reality of Life Among the Pirates.* New York: Random House, Inc., 1995.

Coxere, Edward. *Adventures by Sea of Edward Coxere—A Relation of the Several Adventures by Sea with the Dangers, Difficulties and Hardships I Met for Several Years.* New York and London: Oxford University Press, 1946.

Culver, Henry B. *The Book of Old Ships.* New York: Bonanza Books, 1974.

Dana, Richard Henry, Jr. *The Seaman's Friend—A Treatise on Practical Seamanship.* Boston: Thomas Groom & Co., 1879.

Defense Mapping Agency Hydrographic/Topographic Center. *Red Sea, Bab el Mandeb, Republic of Yemen, Perim Island and Small Strait.* Washington, D.C., 1984.

Dow, George Francis. *Every Day Life in the Massachusetts Bay Colony.* New York: Arno Press, 1977.

An exact narrative of the tryals of the pyrates: and all the proceedings at the late goal-delivery of the Admiralty held in the Old-Bayly on Thursday and Saturday the 7th and 9th of Jan. 1644/45, where eight persons were condemned to die. Ann Arbor, Mich.: University Microfilms, 1978.

Foster, Sir William, ed. *The Red Sea and Adjacent Countries at the Close of the Seventeenth Century as Described by Joseph Pitts, William Daniel, and Charles Jacques Poncet.* London: Oxford University Press, 1949.

Glubok, Shirley, ed. *Home and Child Life in Colonial Days.* Toronto, Ontario: Macmillan Co., 1969.

Gosse, Philip. *The History of Piracy.* New York: Burt Franklin, 1968.

Grey, Charles. *Pirates of the Eastern Seas (1618–1723).* London: Sampson Low, Marston & Co., Ltd., 1933.

Harland, John. *Seamanship in the Age of Sail: An Account of the Shiphandling of the Sailing Man-of-War, 1600–1860.* London: Conway Maritime Press, 1984.

Hill, S. Charles. *Notes on Piracy in Eastern Waters.* Parts 1–6. Bombay: Indian Antiquary, 1923–28.

Hogg, Ian V. *An Illustrated History of Firearms.* New York: A & W Publishers, 1980.

Hoppe, E. O. *Pirates, Buccaneers, and Gentlemen Adventurers.* Cranbury, N.J.: A. S. Barnes and Co., Inc., 1972; London: Thomas Yoseloff, Ltd., 1972.

Humble, Richard. *Ships, Sailors, and the Sea.* New York: Franklin Watts, Inc., 1991.

Ingraham, Leonard W. *An Album of Colonial America.* New York: Franklin Watts, Inc., 1969.

Johnson, Captain Charles [Daniel Defoe]. *A General History of the Robberies and Murders of the Most Notorious Pyrates.* Originally published in 1724. Edited by Manuel Schonhorn. Columbia: University of South Carolina Press, 1972.

Kemp, Peter, ed. *The Oxford Companion to Ships and the Sea.* Oxford: Oxford University Press, 1976.

Lever, Darcy. *The Young Sea Officer's Sheet Anchor—Or a key to the leading of rigging and to practical seamanship.* Originally published in 1819. Mineola, N.Y.: Dover Publications, Inc., 1998.

Marley, David F. *Pirates and Privateers of the Americas.* Santa Barbara, Calif.: ABC-CLIO, Inc., 1994.

McPherson, Kenneth. *The Indian Ocean: A History of People and the Sea.* New Delhi and New York: Oxford University Press, 1993.

Murphy, Dervla. *Muddling Through in Madagascar.* Woodstock, N.Y.: Overlook Press, 1989.

Rediker, Marcus. *Between the Devil and the Deep Blue Sea: Merchant Seamen, Pirates and the Anglo-American Maritime World, 1700–1750.* New York: Cambridge University Press, 1987.

Rogoziński, Jan. *Honor Among Thieves: Captain Kidd, Henry Every, and the Pirate Democracy in the Indian Ocean.* Mechanicsburg, Penn.: Stackpole Books, 2000.

Sherry, Frank. *Raiders and Rebels: The Golden Age of Piracy.* New York: William Morrow & Co., Inc., 1986.

Smith, Carter, ed. *Daily Life—A Sourcebook on Colonial America.* Brookfield, Conn.: Millbrook Press, 1991.

Speare, Elizabeth George. *Life in Colonial America.* New York: Random House, Inc., 1963.

Sydney, William Connor. *England and the English in the Eighteenth Century.* Vols. I and II. Edinburgh: John Grant, 1891.

The Tryals of Joseph Dawson, Edward Forseith, William May, William Bishop, James Lewis, and John Sparkes for several piracies and robberies by them committed: in the company of Every the grand pirate, near the coasts of the East-Indies, and several other places on the seas: giving an account of their villainous robberies and barbarities: at the Admiralty sessions, begun at the Old-Baily on the 29th of October, 1696, and ended on the 6th of November. Ann Arbor, Mich.: University Microfilms, 1980.

Villiers, Alan. *Monsoon Seas: The Story of the Indian Ocean.* New York: McGraw-Hill Book Co., Inc., 1952.

Warwick, Edward, Henry C. Pitz, and Alexander Wyckoff. *Early American Dress: The Colonial and Revolutionary Periods.* New York: Bonanza Books, 1965.

Whitehill, Walter Muir. *Boston: A Topographical History.* Cambridge, Mass.: Belknap Press of Harvard University Press, 1959.